SAM'S JOURNEY

JERRY EBERLY

To: KAREN,

Jerry Eberly

Dageforde Publishing, Inc.

ISBN 1-886225-03-6
Cover design by Pete Smith
Edited by Barbara Sladky

DAGEFORDE
Publishing, inc.

Dageforde Publishing, Inc.
128 East 13th Street
Crete, Nebraska 68333
1-800-216-8794
www.dageforde.com

Printed in the United States of America
10 9 8 7 6 5 4 3 2 1

One

It was a cold, miserable night. A night that was miserable in more ways than one. A part of Jake's life was finally brought to the surface of life that night.

In looking back, his closest friends can understand why Jake was who he was—what he had become.

In Jake's background he was like many of us, a person of the thirties—those tough Depression days that are hard to forget. It seems that the folks of that generation had a few strict, unwritten rules to live by. One in particular that Jake followed was the unwritten rule that in families, especially those of a strong ethnic background, you never discussed the very private situations and problems in your family. Once a problem was solved, or apparently solved, the case was closed forever.

On this particular night in question, Jake was in the hospital with his father, Sam, who was extremely ill. Jake had been spending more and more time with his father this past week. Over a period of a couple of months, Sam's illness had grown worse and worse. This past week had been the worst. Sam had been heavily sedated all week. It was very difficult to watch this once robust, hardworking man waste away before the eyes of his family—day by day.

Because of the sedative, Sam would pass in and out of life's reality. He would talk for long periods of time to his son and then go into his dream world. In his talks with his son, Jake recognized several familiar stories. But in the last few days he heard a couple of new ones.

The day before, after Sam talked about the "old days," he suddenly became still and tears started to roll down his cheeks. Sam reached for his son's hands and held onto them fiercely. He told Jake in an almost weeping voice, "Jacob, your mother and I decided years ago to never tell you about a part of our family history. But now, as my days grow short, I can't keep this from you any longer. Even though your mother and I promised each other that there was no need to tell you about this part of our lives, I feel strongly that I should tell you this story about a piece of your heritage. If I don't tell you, you might never know and I think God will be unhappy with me if I don't."

TWO

At the turn of the twentieth century there were thousands of hopeful immigrants coming to their new home and glorious land of unlimited opportunity—the United States of America.

Most of these people could be telling a very interesting story. They usually had one thing in common—the desire to escape tyranny and horrible living conditions.

At the time a great number of these people were from central Europe: Germany, Poland, Italy, France, and other nearby countries such as Russia.

New York City was the melting pot of all the people arriving in America. The new Americans would naturally find their way to the ethnic community where their native language was spoken.

Sam's first place to settle was in the Williamsburg section of Brooklyn among other German immigrants. After a few weeks he heard that work was available in the shipyards of Philadelphia so he made the move there. He was hired and stayed at a boarding house.

Sam soon met some young men from the shipyards and went to a summer social with them and had a great time—lots of wine, beer, great food, and best of all, several nice young ladies.

It was at this social that Sam met a young man by the name of Ira Weidman, who also worked at the shipyards; from their first meeting they became fast friends.

One night as they told each other stories of their lives, Ira said, "Sam, you tell a good story but where in the heck did you really come from? I know you left something out about your background. I just sense this about you."

Sam replied, "Yes, I suppose you are right, but some things I haven't told you because I really don't want to remember them."

Ira then said, "Sam, we've become good friends, so tell me, where did you come from? I know it is painful to think about. You are similar to my mother and father who fled the Russian pogroms and ghettos as many other Jews did. So my friend, tell me."

Sam said, "I remember the start of my long journey. It began a long, long way from here."

Sam took a long gulp of beer and said, "Many years ago, before I was born, my people were forced again and again to move from village to village. They continually heard the stories of the opportunities in the East.

"At this time my people were trying to survive in southern Germany in the Bavarian area and they became a part of the thousands of people known as the Germans from Russia.

"Over the years in their travels through different countries there were many adjustments to be made. The laws were different, customs were different, and of course, there was a vast difference between the German and Russian languages.

"The Germans were made up of a large variety of peoples. Many times they were divided from other Germans because of their different faiths. There were Lutherans and a mixture of other Protestants, Jews, and of course Catholics. In Russia and Poland it was especially difficult for the Jewish people. In these two countries it was the custom to place all Jews in the Jewish ghetto.

"I was born in the Ukraine area in Russia, in the town of Kavel. I learned early that life would be a struggle and just how mean and cruel our Russian hosts were to the many Germans in Russia. A great threat to my people was the raids by the Russian

Cossacks. They would ride into a village or small town screaming and swearing at everyone in their path. At first notice or warning of the Cossack's coming, the adults would gather all the children and hide them until the intruders finished their pillage and rape of the community."

Sam closed his eyes and remembered, "This was my early childhood. The future looked very bleak. My father and other men began talking more and more about other places where life must be better. He told his family of two places his friends heard about and talked about the most—Palestine and the country to the west—America.

"In the evenings after our meager meal we would gather before the fireplace and listen to our father tell the tales of that place of his dreams, a place of freedom. As children we rarely heard of the word freedom. Every night our father would explain in his simple way what it meant. I thought what a wonderful place America must be.

"One night after we all went to bed, I could not sleep after listening to the stories of that wonderful place. My father was sitting by the fireplace reading his Bible. He noticed me standing there and I went over and sat on the floor beside him. I told him that someday I wanted to go to America and make a good life for myself. My father told me he wanted our whole family to go to America. He said he was making a plan for us. I was the oldest child at fourteen years of age and my father said he would need my help for this great undertaking."

Sam continued, "It was early in the fall and Papa said in a year we would leave here. He said soon he would tell me of his plan and then he sent me to bed. I got up early the next morning, as I did every morning, to help a nearby farmer with his animals, to help support our family. My father left earlier than usual that morning as his job was in a forest close to the other end of our village. His job was cutting down trees with an axe and sometimes a saw for the larger trees. He worked very hard from early morning to late afternoon. Mama told me that Papa went to work early that morning to talk to a man about more work and a chance to make more money."

"I realized right away," Sam continued, "that this was part of Papa's plan to make our trip to America. I knew he would get us there for sure as long as he didn't kill himself by working so hard.

"That night Papa told us about his new extra job. The man he would work for was a trapper and was very successful. Most of his hides and furs were shipped to the larger towns and cities where they were used for hats and coats. Several days a week I was to assist him with the traps in the nearby forest. It would be a lot of hard work, but worth it as we had a glorious goal to meet.

"Soon the weather changed and we had a frigid Russian winter upon us. I look back and wonder how our family survived those long, dreary, cold months. Fortunately our father, in the summer, had all the family help him fill in the cracks of the wooden walls of our house with mud, sod, and twigs mixed together. We did a good job because our poor example of a family home stayed warm and cozy for that horrible winter."

Sam went on to say, "Tending the traps during the cold weather was very hard work. We helped the trapper set the traps for beaver, fox, squirrel, and rabbits. He would also hunt deer and have special hunts for bears. The hunt for the Great Russian bear could be a dangerous activity. A few days after setting the traps we would return to pick up whatever was caught.

"Finally the long winter was over and warmer weather was welcomed by all of us. But with springtime we faced our village streets which became rivers of mud from the melting snow and many rainy days."

Sam added, "One night as we got ready for bed, Papa had me stay up as he wanted to talk to me and my mother. My father said that the next day he was going to visit an old friend in a nearby village. This village, Mojek, was populated by Jewish people by decree of the ruling Cossacks of the area. Papa said that his friend was also planning to leave Russia and had much information and even some maps showing routes to travel through Russia. The difference was that the friend was planning to go to Odessa and then to Palestine.

"Papa said it was getting dangerous to travel to Mojek due to the wild Cossack's stopping and arresting people on the road and entering the Jewish village. Papa told me that if he was detained, I would be the man of the family.

"Papa left early in the morning and avoided the regular road and pathways to Mojek. He walked the several miles, crossing the many fields and making sure that no one saw him. He got to his friend's hovel and after quick greetings they looked over Imel's collection of travel information. The man told him to quickly find what would help him and to make notes on this information. The man said this because his rabbi had found out that the soldiers were going to make a huge raid on them and all men and women from fourteen to thirty would be taken away and probably shipped to Siberia. The rest of them would certainly face either death or hell."

"So," Sam continued, "the visit was cut short and Papa wished his friend well and rushed back to the fields to hike back home. Papa did return home safely and the next day our final plans were determined; in a few days we would leave. Everything was sped up because Papa was afraid the soldiers would leave the Jewish village and attack our village. Papa said we should go about our normal living routine so neighbors would not get any clues about our moving plans."

"The next day," Sam said, "I went early to help the trapper while Papa remained at home to help Mama get things ready for our traveling. I was to tell the trapper my father was ill and could not make it to work. As I arrived at the barn, the trapper was talking to two of his helpers. They seemed nervous in their conversation. I did not pay attention to them and rushed out to do my work in the forest.

"A couple hours later I heard the big trapper yelling at me as he came running toward me. He was out of breath as he stopped and at first it was very hard to understand him. Finally he mumbled out that I must go home. 'There is trouble everywhere as we are all being attacked,' he told me there are large black clouds in the sky near your village and the soldiers are heading this way. Leave now and go across the fields. Be very careful and good luck'.

"As I got closer to our village, I could hardly imagine what was happening. I had heard the horrific stories of past events, but to see the ugliness was hard to believe at first. I finally got to our village and it was hard to recognize anything. Everything seemed to be on fire and smoke was everywhere. I ran and stumbled my way toward the area of our small house. When I got to our neighborhood I looked at all the houses and I wondered where our house was. All the houses, buildings, and sheds were on fire and several were burned to the ground. People were running in circles as obviously no one knew what to do. There were dead people everywhere. I ran into a young man my age and I stopped him as he ran by. Most of his clothes were tattered and burned. I asked him if he had seen my family. His answer was that almost everyone had disappeared. When the raid started he had hid in the potato cellar and when he finally came out he could not find any of his family. The boy said he was leaving. He did not know where, but he would never come back."

Sam continued, "I left the blackened village and spent the night in a haystack outside the village. Early the next morning I went to what I thought was our house. I noticed a part of the small shed in back of our house was still standing. I went to the shed and picked around in the remains. I spotted something shiny under the remains of a small table. After brushing some of the ashes away, I found a small metal box that my mother kept for prized possessions. I grabbed the box and thought I should leave the area immediately before any authorities showed up to create more trouble for the villagers.

"I held on tightly to what I thought, at the time, was my only remaining family possession. I ran back to the same haystack and dug in deep to cover myself. I broke the shiny latch and lock on the box to see what I had recovered. Rolled up in some cloth rags were some neatly scribbled notes with names of relatives—aunts, uncles and unknown cousins. They were neatly listed under the names of villages and towns in Poland and Germany."

Sam added, "To my surprise I found another rolled up cloth rag which held several coins and some paper money—all in German denominations. As a frightened young man with only the clothes on my back and the small metal box, I made my decision to start my big journey. I had heard stories of others making such hard journeys but I had the desire and the fortitude to fight my battles of my young future, so I started my journey to the West."

Three

am drew a breath and after a deep sigh said, "My journey was long, hard and difficult. To this day I do not know how I lived through the experience. I knew from my father's stories and his rough sketches and crude maps that my ultimate goal was to get to the port city of Hamburg. I left the Ukraine village and made my way over several difficult weeks to Radom, Poland. I got work helping a baker late at night and slept in a stable in the hayloft over the horses below.

Sam added, "I discovered in my travels that it was quite easy to find work in a bakery. For some reason bakers always seemed to need a helper to work at night. The pay was usually poor, but I got to eat all the bread and pastries I wanted. I stayed in Radom for two weeks and moved on finally arriving in Lodz, Poland. Again, I got work in a bakery but kept in mind that I should keep moving toward my destination of Hamburg.

"My next travel," Sam continued, "took me to Poznan, Poland and since I had gained some experience I was paid a little more as a baker. It was hard to do, but I kept saving some money. I had no real life to enjoy—it was all work. After a few weeks in Poznan I made my way to Magdeburg, Germany. Finally I was in the home country of my parents and other relatives. In Magdeburg I got work in a Jewish bakery in the ghetto. The people in this city were very nice people and they treated me very well. My boss, the bakery owner, was extremely good to me. He

10

paid me more than I expected. The baker's name was Max Moberg and he was highly respected in the Jewish community."

Sam said, "After working for Max for over a month, he sat down with me and expressed his appreciation for my hard work and loyalty to him. He said he wanted me to stay and work for him for a long time. He was so sincere in talking to me that I did not have the heart to tell him of my plans to move on. I became so happy living in that city that I asked myself why I needed to leave since I had a good life. But I knew of my dream and burning desire to make it to America."

Sam continued, "A couple of days later, Max stopped me after work and said that he wanted me to go with him to meet someone. So we took a short walk to the ghetto to an area where I had never been. I was impressed with what I saw—people all over the sidewalks, visiting and enjoying the day. We stopped in front of an old building made of beautiful stonework. I looked up over the huge main door and saw a large ornamental circle with a blue star inside the circle. I knew I had seen that before, but never paid attention to it. My friend Max put his hand on my shoulder and said that we would go in now. We went into the beautiful interior of the building. There were a few older men sitting on various benches talking to each other and some seemed to be reading to themselves. Max led us to a small table in the front. There was a very large man standing next to the table and Max introduced me to Rabbi David Schplstein. The three of us sat down and had a friendly conversation for several minutes."

Sam paused a bit and then resumed his story. "Max told the Rabbi that he wanted me to meet him because he thought someday I would be in need of some spiritual guidance. They visited a few more minutes and the rabbi told me to drop by anytime to visit and talk. We finished our visit and Max led us out the front door. After taking a few steps, I stopped and asked Max why he had taken me to meet the rabbi. He said that as he had learned more about me, and we had become friends, he thought maybe there was something missing in my life. He thought he could add to my young life and he considered meeting the rabbi to be a gift to me; the rabbi was a great man with much wisdom and a real leader in the community. Max encouraged me to visit the rabbi in the future, but I said, 'Max, I am not a Jew.' Max gave an interesting response, 'Sam, what and who is a Jew? My friend the rabbi is in touch with people of all walks of life. If you are ever in need, see him'."

Ira stood up and said, "Sam, I'm sorry to interrupt your story but I need a stretch and another beer!" They took a break and Sam resumed his adventurous story of getting to America.

"I stayed with Max for a couple more weeks," Sam stated, "and then decided I should head for Hamburg. I finally said goodbye to Max and took off early one morning before the sun came up. Max had helped me get a ride with a peddler for the first part of my trip.

"We traveled over many rough roads in a horse drawn wagon until we got to the peddler's destination. To continue on for the next week I either walked or got lucky and paid a few coins to traveling merchants and peddlers for riding in their wagons.

"Finally," Sam said, "I made my last wagon ride and arrived at the seaport city of Hamburg. For the next few days I walked the waterfront area trying to figure out how to get on one of the huge freighters. Then I noticed other young men getting on ships along the docks. I asked one young man if it was difficult to get on a ship. He said to climb right on and ask permission to speak to whoever hires out basic seamen. He said they were always looking for apprentice seamen.

"I bolstered my courage and climbed up the gangplank on the largest vessel on the waterfront. I was finally shown to the quarters of the boatswain who was in charge of hiring out seamen. He was friendly and somehow knew that I was looking for work. When I told him that I had experience as a baker he smiled and said to report back to him in two days and that I would be hired to help the head baker. Then he shook my hand and welcomed me aboard the *Deutsche Rhinegold*."

Sam added, "I left with a huge feeling of relief—I was finally on my last step to America. The German freighter departed the harbor for the open seas three days later. I worked hard every day in the galley, but I was thrilled to be on my way to America. After many, many days at sea we docked in the harbor of New York City. I signed off the freighter and with my meager belongings headed for the streets to celebrate my arrival in this big wonderful country of America."

Sam took a deep breath and said, "Ira, I did not mean to ramble on for such a long time, but that was my journey to America—and here I am an American!"

Four

Ira Weidman also had an interesting background. As a young man he secured a job at a Philadelphia shipyard working as a painter. He proved to be a hard worker and his foreman recognized Ira's abilities and soon gave him more responsibilities. With the additional experience he decided to look for ways to improve his income. He was very ambitious and also very smart.

One day he went to the owner of the tenement where he lived and worked out a deal to do painting for the landlord. He worked long hours during the week at the shipyard and painted apartments on weekends and in his spare time.

After several weeks of this Ira saw an opportunity to leave the shipyards and develop his own small painting business. Ira's hard work paid off as he became successful in just a few months.

One evening Ira visited Sam and told him he had developed his own paint business to the point that he was in need of good, dependable help. So far his helpers were part-time and not very good workers.

After discussing the situation with Sam, Ira talked Sam into going to work for him. They laid out a plan and Sam left the shipyard and went to work as a painter. Ira's judgment about Sam was right. The two worked well together and Sam proved to be an honest and loyal worker, as well as a true friend.

As the days and weeks passed, the business grew. Word spread that the man to see about painting was the guy at Weidman Paint Company in the Fairmont Park area of Philadelphia.

The two young men worked hard during the week so by the end of the week they were ready to relax and take it easy. These two men were handsome and fit. Many young ladies in the community were eager to join them socially.

At one summer get-together at a nice park on the Schuylkill River, Sam met Ira's cousin, Dan Favinger, another nice young man. The three became close friends.

Ira told his two pals that his lady friend would be at the park that day at a family picnic and that she would have two girl friends with her. She naturally encouraged Ira to bring a couple of nice fellows along to meet her friends.

What a delightful get-together it was! Cupid personally had an eager hand in the meeting of these three couples and they paired off naturally.

Ira's sweetheart was Sarah who had long reddish-blonde hair and gray-hazel eyes, and was quite short in stature.

Sam believed he had just met the beauty of his life. Her name was Rina. She had jet black hair and pretty, bright blue eyes and was a little taller than the other two girls.

Dan was introduced to Lela, a blonde with blue eyes who had a very cheerful disposition—always a smile on her face.

The three young couples had a wonderful time together and when the evening ended, they all agreed to get together the next weekend.

Ira had become very successful with his business and therefore quite comfortable financially so he felt he was in a position to ask for Sarah's hand in marriage. Because of their backgrounds it was important that they respect tradition in making a marriage pact. The marriage plans were announced several months after their first meeting.

Ira had been extremely nervous about meeting Sarah's father. The man who was originally from southern Germany was known to be tough. He was a successful businessman, and with Sarah being his youngest daughter, he was somewhat overprotective of her. But, he gave his blessing to the happy couple and they were married two months later.

Cupid was consistent and within six months both Sam and Dan proposed and married their sweethearts.

Dan was a real natural at dealing with people. For a while he was a successful salesman in the clothing department of a large department store.

Ira suggested that Dan look into getting into the insurance business. Dan followed up on this idea and decided to give it a try. Sure enough, after some training and experience Dan became a real champ in the insurance business. His specialty was selling life policies to low-income families at a fee of twenty-five cents a week. Dan not only sold the policies, but he also did the collecting of the premiums. Soon he was selling all types of insurance policies.

Within a year and a half Dan was one of the top salesmen in the company. His boss said, "I'm not sure how you are doing so good—but keep doing it, whatever it is!"

Sam and Rina were content with married life. Rina worked in a women's clothing store and enjoyed her job. Sam was also content with his job and liked working for Ira, who was a great boss.

But, Sam felt that something was missing in his life. He truly believed that the good Lord had more for him to do than painting houses and barns. Sam never discussed these innermost feelings with Rina, but once in a while Rina saw Sam daydreaming and his mind traveling to some far away place. Finally, one weekend while having a picnic at a park with friends, Rina noticed Sam was mentally away—somewhere in another world. She asked Sam to take a walk along the river.

After a few minutes, Rina sat down with her husband and encouraged him to speak out and let her into his dreams and his thoughts. Sam said that he was sorry if he had been evasive recently and did not mean to be distant to her.

Sam was an avid reader and every day he bought a local paper for two cents on his way home. During the evening he would take time to read the paper from front to back. Sam told Rina that in reading more and more he became fascinated about the wonders and opportunities that were available in America.

As his imagination grew, he also thought what possibilities there were for Rina and him. Sam was a dreamer of adventurous things but he was also a doer. Like many other young men of this era, Sam was reading and hearing stories about the movement to the western part of our country. A large number of these people were the immigrants living in the eastern part of America—people just like Sam.

So, Sam talked of his imagined adventures and he told Rina that they should think about making a move to the western part of the country. Rina could hardly believe what her husband was saying. She had lived in a big city all her life and could not imagine what the wild west was like. But Sam was so positive in his thinking and assured his young wife that he would not do anything impossible or make a decision without her consent. They decided to study the move west and to gather all the information they could about opportunities available.

Over the next several months they discussed the West with many different people who had facts about the growth, the prosperity, and also the hardships in that part of the country.

One day, Sam read an article in the paper about people who were making their future in the West. At the end of the article it directed readers to the last page of the paper for a listing of opportunities available at the time. Sam quickly turned to the last page. There was a complete listing of the many opportunities working for the railroad out west. Men who were serious-minded and hardworking were needed. If interested a man would apply for work, transportation could be arranged for him if he were accepted.

Sam and Rina sat down and reviewed all the information they had gathered and formed a plan. They discussed it for a couple of months and finally made a decision. Their plan was to have Sam go west by himself to establish a base for the two of them. After a time, if things were not right, then Sam would return to Philadelphia. If things were good, then Rina would make the trip west.

Sam made his commitment to the railroad and the business office scheduled Sam's trip and gave him a pass to make the trip west.

Sam left Rina and started the long trip west. On the trip Sam had a few layovers and it was an educational experience seeing other cities and new areas of America. Sam was truly amazed at the vastness of his country. He felt it was a privilege to be a part of this great country. He was very proud and excited about his future.

Five

After a one-day lay over in Chicago, Sam was sent on to Omaha where he would get his first work assignment. He arrived in Omaha in early spring and there was still some snow on the ground. At first he worked on a crew that repaired the tracks. After a week he was called in for a talk with his supervisor—a huge Irishman. He told Sam that he was being trained to eventually run a track repair crew out in the western part of Nebraska.

The Irishman had a real Irish brogue and had a fine taste for his country's beer and whiskey. Sam continually turned down invitations from Paddy the Irishman to visit a popular Irish pub. Paddy and his Irish buddies were a fun loving group and didn't understand Sam's not wanting to booze the evening away. In spite of their differences on drinking, the two became close friends.

Paddy told Sam that many men who immigrated from Ireland got their first jobs building railroads all across America. It was a real opportunity for them, especially when they remembered the severe hardships of living in Ireland where there were few opportunities to improve themselves.

There was another ethnic group that Sam quickly learned about in his work with the railroad—the Chinese. Sam found these people to be so different from any other people he had known. At the start of the century the railroads and other businesses needed more cheap labor for their many developments in the western part of the country. At this time there was terrible turmoil in China. The people of China were being torn apart politically. On May 31, 1900, the Boxer Rebellion started its way through China. If the revolutionaries thought someone did not agree with them, he was murdered on the spot.

Because of these horrible conditions thousands of Chinese men left for America and were willing to work for bare minimum wages. The railroad companies hired thousands of these Chinese men to lay the track lines across the country. The goal of many of the Chinese men was to save money and eventually return to their homeland—when their country finally returned to more peaceful times. Many of these workers entered America illegally on ships that landed on the west coast and the railroad eagerly hired them for the back-breaking job of laying the track for hundreds and hundreds of miles.

Most of the white men like Sam were given the softer (if there was such a thing) jobs on the track line, while the Chinese did all the pick and shovel work.

During the warmer months of the year many men slept in the fields along the side of the tracks. In harsher weather they spent their nights in boxcars.

As the rail lines moved farther and farther west, more and more small towns and villages began to spring up out of nowhere.

Some of the Chinese decided to take on part-time jobs in some of the larger towns along the track lines. They worked as dishwashers, cooks, shoe shiners, and laundrymen.

Sam was also looking for extra work whether it was with the railroad or another company. He believed any extra money would make things better and shorten the time he and Rina were apart.

The railroad line finally worked its way to the vast open prairie land in western Nebraska. The railroad chose a particular town as the site for its centralized operation point for the growing railroad business. The chosen town was growing and was a key area for the cattle business which at the time was very important to the area economy.

As time went on, Sam came to the conclusion that he did not want to work on the railroad forever. Therefore, Sam began to study the different men in town who had worked hard and became successful. These various men were from all walks of life but they were all very tough men—physically as well as mentally. They also had one other common characteristic—the strong desire to succeed. Some of these men were honest in their makeup. Some were not so honest and at times very brutal to almost everyone.

Sam was getting very homesick for his wife. Things were not moving along fast enough for him according to his original plan. So, he figured he would have to take some bold steps to speed things along to bring his young wife out to the vast prairie land.

Over the long days and weeks working on the track line, Sam who was one of the few white men to go out of his way to get with men from different ethnic backgrounds, became acquainted with Lee Chin, a Chinese man whose English was very limited. In spite of the language barrier the two young men got along well with each other and Sam continually helped Lee with his English. But, after a while Sam lost track of his new friend and after asking around, he was told that Lee had left the railroad.

Meanwhile, Sam had found a part-time job on weekends at a shoe repair shop owned by a Greek fellow. Sam's job was to clean up and polish shoes and cowboy boots.

One weekend Sam heard a couple of cowboys talking about the fine Chinese meal they had just consumed. Sam interrupted his work to ask about where they got this Chinese food. The cowboys said the small café was just down the street and around the corner in the basement of a building.

When Sam got off work, he walked to the small café. He saw a homemade sign hanging in front of the stairway entry to the small café. The sign said "Lee's China." Sam said to himself, Bingo! That must be my friend in there.

Sam's Journey

Sam walked into the small place and there was Lee at a table near the kitchen counting money in a couple of cigar boxes. The café was small but there were about twenty customers there. Sam noticed that all the workers were men, there was not one woman and Sam thought this a bit odd.

Lee looked up from his counting and jumped for joy when he saw his friend Sam. After giving his friend a big welcome hug, he took Sam to his small office in back of the kitchen where they shared some tea.

Lee told Sam a shortened version about his leaving the railroad as he had to get back to work; but he promised to tell Sam more later. Lee told how he saved every penny he could to fulfill his dream of a café in America—his new beautiful country. Only in America could he do such a thing.

Lee had a rich (or well-to-do anyway) uncle who had a successful laundry business in Denver. Their total family members were executed by the Revolutionaries in China. The uncle, Woo Chinn, had very strong feelings for his nephew and would do what he could for Lee to be happy and successful.

This uncle made a trip to see Lee for a couple of days. These two men were the only survivors of their family. After visiting for a time, Lee told his uncle of his desire to own a café. He explained it was a dream of his, but he had a problem financing the project. No matter how much money he saved he could not get enough to make a deal for his dream café. At this time there were few banks who would lend to any young Chinese man.

The older gentleman listened to his nephew's tale of discouragement. Finally the old man said, "Let me think this through. I will help you make a plan for your future."

"But how?" asked Lee.

The old man said, "I will have an answer for your worry and discontent, all in proper Chinese fashion. Now, read your tea leaves and say a nice prayer."

The next morning at breakfast Uncle Woo told Lee that their new country had been good to him. Woo also experienced trouble getting started, but due to a little luck and hard work he was a success. He had been in America for fifteen years now and said he had been able to save a few dollars and had made a few investments with other immigrants.

Then Uncle Woo explained how he would put together the financing for Lee's project. He was willing to lend the money to his nephew and to be a partner in the café business. Uncle Woo's business experience was an enormous help in setting up the café operation.

The uncle returned to Denver and organized his business organization so that he could spend a month with his nephew in getting the café running in a positive way. The first two weeks were slow at the new café. After Lee made visits around town to promote himself and the café, things began to pick up. Most of his customers were Chinese and black men working on the railroad. His cooks and waiters were all Chinese men. They all stayed working on the railroad and worked part-time for Lee.

Soon word got around town about the good meals and popular prices at Lee's China Café. Lee lived a very frugal life and saved most of his money.

In their conversation Sam said he was envious of Lee's independence and success. Sam told his friend he wanted that same ingredient in his life—independence—and he wanted that opportunity to prove to himself that he could be a success in his life.

Lee listened to his friend and sensed his frustration. Lee finally asked, "What do you want to do? Since I was a boy, I was always interested in food and cooking and I soon knew that the café business was for me."

Sam explained that from meeting several cowboys he became interested in their work and lifestyle. As he became friends with a couple of these rough, tough men, they invited him out to where they worked. The cowboys did this because they knew he was truly interested in how they worked and being from the East it was a fascinating lifestyle to him.

Sam's Journey

Sam and one of the cowboys, Willy, became close buddies. As Sam asked more and more questions, Willy was always the one who gave the best answers. Willy taught Sam how to rope and ride and how to handle cattle. He also told Sam he would make a good cowpuncher.

Lee told Sam he should get into the cattle business. The two friends talked this through and Lee said he wanted to get advice from his Uncle Woo and maybe they could work out a Chinese deal which brought out some laughter. Lee said his uncle was expanding his business ventures and had become a very respected man in the big city of Denver. Because of his uncle's interest in seeking new investments, Lee thought he might be interested in helping Sam get started. Lee also told Sam that he would help with the financing because then he would have a good supplier of beef for his café.

Lee also told Sam that in his personal philosophy of life he believed in helping a good friend. Then jokingly he said he might even make a buck out of the deal.

Sam's friend became quiet for a few minutes and Sam knew that meant the man had something serious on his mind.

Lee finally said, "I must tell you something that may cause worry. If we support your business venture, we must be very quiet about where any money comes from or where it goes. You must never tell anyone about me or my uncle helping you financially because we are in this country illegally. Like many Chinese in this country, we had to leave China to save our lives, leaving family members there.

"My uncle has had to make many payoffs and provide 'gifts' to the correct people to be successful in his business life. In doing all this, he has a few silent business partners with whom he shares his income. If the wrong people hear too much about us and our success, we could be deported. Many Americans don't realize their Senate voted for a Chinese Exclusion Act to keep cheap Chinese labor out of the country. This ruling was made due to the fear that Americans would lose jobs to cheap Chinese labor.

This threat is always there for people like me, so, be careful about the deal we are planning. I know of several Chinese men who have been deported to Mexico."

Lee then added, "In my uncle's business connections he became involved in some transactions that were illegal, and because of those ventures he is in too deep to get out. So, you and I must keep our business dealings legitimate all the way and not let anyone else get involved with us."

Sam did not know what to think of all this. He told his friend that maybe he should forget the whole deal.

Lee told Sam he did not mean to chase him away or discourage him. He said his whole life had been a big gamble and that he and his uncle accepted this as a way of life for them. He merely told his friend, "Don't give up. I'll help you fight your battle, so be brave."

Sam appreciated his friend being up front with him. He knew Lee was a true friend and would fight to the end for him. Sam couldn't have asked for a better business partner.

Uncle Woo came for another visit and after hearing Sam's plans for raising cattle, he agreed to help finance the project. Sam quit the railroad and started his new adventure in America.

Six

By now the Homestead Act was in full swing allowing many immigrants to gain ownership of land. Sam was one of many who took advantage of this opportunity to secure his first few hundred acres of land. He was required to build a dwelling on the homestead claim, so Sam's cowboy friend, Willy, helped to build a small cabin which served as his first home on his land.

A small pen was put together to hold his first few head of cattle and Willy helped Sam buy a couple of cow ponies. After several weeks Sam was making progress in becoming a capable rancher.

One day, after a hard day's work, Sam met with Willy and they discussed the growth of the small ranch. Willy, with a lot of cowpuncher experiences, patted his friend on the back and told him he was very proud of him. Sam replied that he was proud of himself and that the ranch was the guiding star of his life and he was now going back east to get his wife.

Willy suggested that should be the name of his ranch—the Star Ranch. Sam liked the idea so he named his wonderful piece of America "The Star Ranch."

Sam knew from experience that living conditions would be harsh and a different experience for his wife. So in his next letter to Rina he painted a fairly negative picture of what life on the prairie would be like.

Rina wrote right back to Sam and told him not to worry. Together they would accomplish their goal. Rina had a very adventurous spirit and assured Sam that she was eager to make the trip West. She also let him know she was very lonesome for him and that they had been apart long enough.

Sam's ranch had become quite a success and he hired his friend Willy as a regular ranch hand. Sam put Willy in charge of the ranch while he went east to get his wife.

Before leaving on his trip east, Willy suggested they begin building a small sod house near the cabin he was living in. Willy had some cowboy pals help in building the sod house but the construction went slow as they only worked part-time.

During his days in the west, Sam had made connections with all kinds of people. A few became good friends and many others were friendly business contacts. One positive factor for Sam was that he was well respected by all.

Since Sam was well respected, he had no trouble making a deal with the railroad manager when it came time to arrange transportation to Philadelphia. The manager valued Sam and his business ability and also was sure Sam was going to be a big time success in the near future, therefore an asset to the railroad on the local level of business.

Sam left Nebraska on a nice summer day. After several days of travel, Sam was greeted at the Philadelphia depot by Rina and their friends the Weidmans and the Favingers. There was a party that evening with friends and relatives and they were up late as Sam told many stories about the wild west and the growth of America.

After a few days, Sam and Rina decided it was time to leave for their home in Nebraska. As their train trip moved on mile after mile, Rina became more and more amazed at the beauty of our country. Sam had tried to prepare her for the breathtaking scenery, but to actually see it firsthand was more than she could imagine.

Sam's Journey

When they arrived, Rina was again surprised at the vast wide-open country and at the end of that day she witnessed her first sunset which was so beloved by westerners. The beautiful, glorious colors spread across the sky as far as the eye could see. It was a true picture made only by God. That experience made Rina truly fall in love with this new prairie home of hers.

Finally, on an early morning, the train pulled into the town that would be their home for many years.

Willy met them at the depot and they picked up their several suitcases and boxes and loaded them onto the ranch wagon. They then headed northwest to their ranch. The wagon ride was a bumpy five-mile trek over gulleys and hills.

They came to a small rise of the prairie and at the top Willy stopped the wagon. Before them was a small valley and about a quarter of a mile into the valley Sam pointed out their small house and other outbuildings, the ponds and streams that ran through their land in the surrounding area. The area had been described in letters from Sam, but his words did not do justice to the wonderful sight viewed by Rina. Sam, with much joy in his voice, said to Rina, "Just think, this is ours."

As they slowly came down the rise, Sam noticed a few people gathered around their ranch home. Willy said, "I guess we have some visitors." Some neighbors and friends were waiting to greet them as they got off the wagon. A crude paper banner spread across the front of the cabin with the words "Welcome Rina." There were also tables filled with food and drinks set up around the yard.

In one big voice, everyone gave Rina a huge welcome to Nebraska. There was much backslapping and friendly handshaking. To say the least, Rina was thrilled with this wonderful welcome and very impressed with these warm, friendly people.

Sam finally noticed that something was very different. He went over to the small cabin and found that the sod house had been built right into one side of the cabin. This made the small house double in size. Part of the sod house was not finished, but it was very livable. Sam knew right away what had happened and he immediately turned and grabbed his friend Willy to thank him and express his appreciation for all his hard labor and workmanship.

"Willy, this is wonderful," Sam told him, "but however did you manage this all by yourself?"

Willy knew his friend was happy with the improvements and quickly answered, "It was not just me. Several of us here helped out. We made the work into a small labor of love for two of our neighbors. Someday you can return the favor. This is a part of our western culture and appreciation for each other."

One of the old cowboys had brought his guitar and after they finished eating dinner the cowboy started strumming a tune. Dancing and singing went on into the evening. As the guests prepared to leave, Sam got to his feet by the campfire and thanked everyone for coming and for all they had done in welcoming Rina to her new home. The friends and neighbors felt Sam's sincerity and warm feelings toward them.

Something magical happened that night. Sam connected with all those people that night in a very emotional way. Young and old, they all left knowing that here was a very special man who would help lead them to a promising, bright future.

"I was surprised and uplifted by your words, Sam," Willy told his friend.

"Thank you, but I did not mean to impress anyone. I was only saying what I felt and what was true."

"They were remarkable words, dear," Rina said as she approached them. "Sounds like you could be turning into a politician." Sam laughed at her remark.

Sam and Rina looked forward to their first night together in their new home and Rina thought of the joy she would have in unpacking their possessions in the following days.

Seven

The next day Willy said, "Sam, I had an important visitor while you were gone. A well-known cattleman, probably the largest rancher in the area, came for a visit. The man arrived on horseback with two mean-looking cowboys, who were wearing six-shooters on their hips. I worried about what was in store for me.

"The 'top man' wore a ten-gallon hat and a handsome pair of black leather chaps. He was sitting on a beautiful jet black stallion. The man got off his horse and introduced himself as Cyrus Dutman, a neighbor. He told me his ranch is north and east of here and his brand is CY-1 marker.

"The man was large, more than six feet tall, and as wide as a bull. I noticed that there was an accent in the man's speech, but I could not identify the ethnic tone of it."

This was not new, of course, as most people in this western area were immigrants, and mostly from a European culture. The large rancher had a very commanding presence about him that made him appear very authoritative.

Willy added, "Cyrus Dutman told me that he was looking for Mr. Samuel Rignez and wanted to talk business with him. I told Dutman you were gone and we agreed that you would meet in town upon your return. We arranged a time that you would meet with Dutman at Lee Chinn's Chinese Café."

In the days before the meeting, Sam and Willy gathered as much information as they could about Cyrus Dutman. They found out that he was an honest, hard-working rancher. He came to the area as a young cowboy and started out on a small homestead. He continually picked up more land and developed a large herd of cattle.

They found out that at the time Dutman first started in the area, it was sparsely settled and quite lawless. The six-shooter and the Winchester ruled the vast prairie country. No one could prove anything, but it was believed that Dutman made his own justice in those early days. A few bad characters, rustlers, and horse thieves who did Dutman wrong simply disappeared overnight after their experience with this rugged individual. Another rancher summed up the man: If you deal with him, be careful at all times and know where his hands are.

On the day that Sam and Dutman were to meet, Dutman made it to the café ten minutes early. After entering Lee's place, he and his two cowboys walked through the place, not missing anything that could later be a surprise to him.

Sam and Willy arrived a couple minutes later. Dutman pulled a watch from a vest pocket and said, "I admire and value you being on time. That is important to me."

The five men sat at a corner table and Lee guided all the other customers away from that corner of the café.

Dutman quickly looked over the area and got right to the point. "Don't be alarmed with me," he said. I know many people have a fear of me. I don't know why. My past life has been a tough struggle. I have had to fight hard every day from the time I was sixteen years old. Through hard work and some luck I have been quite successful. This is a rugged country and if you fight the good battle, a cowboy like me can amount to something.

"But I have made some enemies and I am getting to the age where I want to slow down a bit. My dear wife has had to put up with many hardships being married to me and I want to make things easier for her. We raised two daughters out here in this wild country and they have become real ladies. We have not been blessed with any sons. At this time, I would like these good men to leave you and me for some private talk."

After the three men left, Dutman told Sam, "I have been watching and studying you for some time. There is a young attorney in town who does legal work for me and I had him check out your background. He found you to be an honest and fair man and also aggressive in your business dealings."

Sam started to speak, but the big man told him to stay calm and just listen. He said, "We are both very much alike. I believe we both originally came from the same area of the Old Country and I have a gut feeling that we can get along.

"As I've told you, I want to slow down quite a bit and frankly I need some help. I would like to make an arrangement with you. I have thought this through and I think you are the one man I can trust. I want to share in the management of our two ranches."

Dutman added, "Right now we are both facing a problem. It might be a small problem now, but we must correct it before it gets out of hand. And I do believe you and I are the ones to solve it. We should do this not just for ourselves, but for all the nearby farmers and ranchers.

"I have discovered two bad, bad hombres who are fairly new to the area and have formed a small gang. For the past three months they have been stealing a few head of cattle here and there, but they are now getting greedy and quite bold. They recently stole a few from me including a favorite bull and I won't put up with this.

"My two top wranglers who are here with me today have followed these varmint thieves around the area and have found out where they hang out near the South Lake area. This group seems to have a fairly smart leader, but he has finally outsmarted himself.

"One problem we have," Dutman added, "is that the marshal of this region is not scheduled to be here for nearly another three weeks and we can't wait three weeks. By the way, our marshal is from the south area in the Oklahoma Territory and I'm told he is a relative of Judge Roy Bean—the 'hanging judge' from the southwest region. So, our marshal has the right connections."

Sam sat back in his chair, absorbing Dutman's words.

Dutman continued, "Sam, we are talking about two things here, our potential partnership and correcting a harm on our land that affects many others. I'll give you time to think about being partners, but I hope you will join me in solving this problem we are faced with. My plan would be to surprise them right at sunrise just before they wake up. I have twenty men available to make our raid. How many men can you round up?"

Sam replied, "I have seven good men, but I will have to talk to them first. I need to know that we will be obeying the law on this raid."

Dutman said, "Sam, I've been through this before and the men I've learned from years before taught me that without a legal lawman around when needed, the 'law of the range' takes over. We will make our justice fair and quick, and that is all there is to it. That's my answer to you. Let me know tomorrow if you will join me. I have some Lakota Tribe members that live on the edge of my property. I have their men work for me off and on throughout the year. They're good people and very loyal to me. Many people in our area hardly know they exist but that is the way the Lakota want it."

Dutman ended the meeting and Sam went back to his ranch to discuss the situation with Rina.

The next day, Sam decided he had an obligation to work with Dutman on eliminating the rustlers.

Dutman scheduled a meeting for the next day for all the men involved. Sam was impressed with all the men meeting at the Dutman ranch. They represented many ethnic groups and were in all shapes and sizes. One thing Sam noticed was that all of Dutman's men were very large, many more than six feet tall, and heavily muscled.

The plan was to ride to the rustlers' camp in two days. Dutman had two of his men spend twenty-four hours a day spying on the rustlers' camp and watching their every move.

Soon, the day of the raid came. The last thing Dutman did was to give two wranglers' ropes four feet in length to each cowboy. When they put the rustlers together, Dutman would have them bound tightly with the lengths of rope. Dutman had made arrangements to use two old barns outside of town to keep the rustlers in as a temporary jail while waiting for the marshal to arrive.

Halfway to the rustlers' camp they met Dutman's two spying cowboys who reported that there were twelve thieves in the gang, all very wild and boisterous. Every night they would get stupid drunk and usually have several fights. There were some tents and a couple of lean-tos they used while some of them slept on the ground.

Dutman gathered his men together a couple hundred yards from the rustlers' camp. He split the men into four groups and decided they would approach the camp from four different directions and would completely surround the bad guys. The men would leave their horses about thirty yards from the camp and quietly approach the sleeping men.

The first concern was to find where the rustlers had their guns. After locating the guns near the sleeping bandits, Dutman gave the command to secure the enemy.

Their timing was perfect. Dutman's signal to attack was by shooting his shotgun into the air. The roar of the shotgun blast awakened the sleeping men and scared them to death. The cowboys then forced the rustlers to their knees around the campfire where they were securely tied with ropes.

Dutman had a hardwood stick three feet long that was covered with leather and was as hard as steel. Normally he used this as a cattle prod, but it was also used as a weapon when needed.

The group of rustlers was screaming and cursing for some explanation about what was going on. They also wanted to know who these tough guys were. There was no doubt that Dutman was running this show of problem-solving on the prairie.

Dutman had found out days before who the gang leader was; he was very competent in digging up information about all types of people. Later, many important leaders said that Dutman could and should have been the number one lawman in the region because of this ability to gather the basic facts and information.

The ringleader's name was Mac Bruner. He was previously known as a bad dude from the Oklahoma Territory. Dutman had Bruner brought to the front of the group close to the campfire. He had one of his men remove the rope from Bruner's legs. Bruner screamed and cussed Dutman who told the man, "From now on shut your big mouth and don't say a word until you are told to."

Bruner screamed back with several obscenities, "You're no one to tell me anything."

Dutman walked to the man and swung his cattle prod and connected with the man's left ear and the ear was half ripped off and blood flew everywhere. Bruner fell to the ground like a rock and never made a move.

The rustlers made one long moan as if by one man. Dutman raised his shotgun and fired a blast to the sky and said to the rustlers, "You asked who we are. I'll tell you now, we are the ranchers and farmers whose cattle you stole. You're through around here forever, you are going to face our marshal. You will go to town peacefully or you'll be dropped out here just like this rotten example of a man was dropped."

Dutman and Sam organized the rustlers in a single line and prepared to hike them to town. He left five of the top wranglers there to start holding the stolen cattle to a point where they could drive them to the town's sale barn pens. The ranchers and farmers could then come to the sale barn and claim their animals.

They also took the rustler's horses with them and had them penned at the sale barn.

The whole episode was accomplished quickly and without any fanfare at all. The men that participated never talked about the experience. Dutman told them to never tell stories about it, and the men did not want to do anything that could get them on the wrong side of Cyrus Dutman.

But, as it happens in life so many times, the whole story leaked out in bits and pieces; maybe a cowboy slipped up and told a wife or girlfriend and she repeated the story. When the story was repeated, it was done in hushed tones for, again, no one wanted to meet up with Cyrus Dutman and face his fierce anger.

After a couple of weeks, all of the cattle had been returned to their owners and the marshal appeared. Some very reputable businessmen met with Dutman and the marshal to explain how the cattle had been recovered. Sam was also invited to this meeting. It was believed by the group that it was time to get some younger responsible men involved in the more serious concerns of the area—especially when enforcing the law.

The marshal was Gil Zachman, a very reputable lawman with an outstanding record in the great southwest. He spent most of his time in the Oklahoma Territory. Fortunately, Zachman had become a good friend of Cyrus Dutman. Dutman and his group told their story and the marshal backed them up.

They took the marshal to the barns where the rustlers were held. These guys were not in the best of shape, Zachman pointed out.

Dutman said, "We did the best we could. We fed them two times a day and we hosed them down with the village fire truck. That was humane treatment as far as we were concerned. Now they are your problem."

Two days later the marshal deputized some tough cowboys to assist him in loading the rustlers in a railroad cattle car and taking them to an eastern city for a trial.

At the time of their departure, Dutman appeared to witness their leaving. The ringleader, Mac Bruner, spotted Dutman and screamed obscenities at him. Dutman ignored him until Bruner yelled, "I'll be back and you and your family will pay for my misery!"

Dutman exploded within himself. He slowly boarded the cattle car carrying his cattle prod in his belt on his backside. He approached Bruner and said, "Those were your last words you will speak to me and never will you speak anything to my family." At that instant, Dutman pulled his cattle prod from his belt and swung it up and against the right side of Bruner's head, cutting it severely and making a bloody mess. Bruner hit the floor in a lump and was unconscious. Dutman quietly left the cattle car and went with his two cowboys to return to his ranch.

What an example of old West justice!

Eight

After this ordeal came to a close, people felt that Cyrus Dutman was their hero and could handle anything and everything in their town.

As time went on Dutman and Sam became closer and closer. Soon the two men met and agreed to have a loose-knit partnership—and that is what it was, loosely organized but the two men felt comfortable with the agreement.

Dutman had his lawyer write up some legal papers that the two agreed on and they shook hands; that was that. A big announcement was never made, but local people, especially ranchers, just knew a tight bond was created.

After the legal agreement was made, Sam said they should celebrate with their wives. Sam and Rina invited Cyrus and his wife, Anna, for dinner. Sam arranged for Lee Chinn to prepare a celebration dinner and what a great time the two couples had.

The relationship that developed between Anna and Rina was especially good for Anna. She had no other real women friends. She had married Cyrus as a young girl, just fifteen years old. Anna's life was made up of work, work, and work and she was always tied up on the prairie and the ranch. Her life had been very harsh, which was true at that time for many women living in the high plains country.

Although Rina had learned to love her new life and the ranch and the high plains country, her new friendship with Anna added great joy to her life.

Late one evening, Rina met Sam out near the corral as he was putting his saddle away. She told him she had a surprise for him. Rina sang out in a happy voice, "Sam, I do believe next spring you are going to be blessed with a wonderful child—I'm pregnant!"

She went on and told him how she had visited Anna that day and Anna helped her figure out what her situation was. Being her first pregnancy, she said she just wasn't sure and not being close to a doctor she needed some assurance.

Sam was filled with instant joy and whooped and hollered so loud that he frightened their sheep dog away from the yard. They made plans to go to town the next day to visit Dr. Brown, the only doctor in the area.

Dr. Herman Brown had a lot in common with Sam. He, like so many in the area, had come from the East. He grew up in New Jersey so he knew about Philadelphia and many of Sam and Rina's old haunts and neighborhoods.

Dr. Brown often told Sam and Rina that he was so happy and content living in the West compared to the big eastern cities. He cited how, as many immigrants did, because of prejudices and anti-Semitic feelings, his father changed their name from Braunstein to Brown. Dr. Brown's father believed this change would hide his family's background and help them become Americanized.

Dr. Brown examined Rina and assured her and Sam that she was healthy and that they should have a healthy baby. The doctor told Rina that as the months went by, she should take better care of herself and the baby because of the distance the ranch was from town. Sam promised the doctor he would take good care of his wife.

Sam's Journey

As the months went by many friends in the area made visits to Rina and Sam's to congratulate them and of course the women with children gave plenty of advice concerning babies.

In the early spring, after a long, hard winter, Dr. Brown made a visit. He had not seen Rina for a while and thought she might be more comfortable in town staying with friends because it was getting close to her time. Rina turned the idea down as she wanted to be with Sam and stay on the ranch which she truly loved. By now, they had developed the ranch into a very comfortable and livable place. Everyone was very impressed with the way the couple had improved their home, mostly because of Rina's imagination and hard work.

Three weeks later, Rina went out for her usual afternoon walk. She had a couple of trails she followed and really loved the new spring wildflowers and the welcomed warm weather.

She was walking east of the house and was approaching an old barn Sam used for storage. There was also an Indian style tent beside the barn put up by some Indian folks who were friendly to Sam and Rina.

All of a sudden labor pains quickly hit Rina. She knew what they were, but it still surprised her. Another couple of contractions came to her and she staggered to the side of the trail and dropped to her knees.

Fortunately at the same time Willow Tall Tree was just coming over a rise on the trail toward Rina. Willow was returning from town with some supplies in the back of her wagon and had planned to stop and see Rina and to give her some baby clothes.

Willow had become an unofficial midwife in the area, assisting Dr. Brown in the birth of many babies. She parked her wagon, jumped down quickly, and helped Rina into the nearby teepee. There was a large pile of burlap sacks in the teepee and she piled several to make a place for Rina to lie down.

Willow, in her singsong voice, sang an old Lakota lullaby to help Rina relax. Within an hour or so a handsome baby boy was born. Willow used an old flour sack, which was all that was available to wrap the little baby and handed him to his mother.

After resting for a while, Rina was able to get up and Willow assisted her into the wagon and to the ranch house a short distance away. She helped Rina and the baby to bed where they both fell into a deep sleep.

As the early evening approached, Willow was sitting on the porch and saw Sam and Willy riding in over a nearby hilltop. They pulled up in front of the house and received a hearty welcome and the announcement of the baby's arrival. The three of them rushed to the bedroom where Rina was waking from her deep slumber.

Willow had to return to her village and said she would soon return with a couple of young women to help Rina for a few days. For that evening, ever faithful Willy cooked the evening meal while Sam took care of his wife and son.

During the next several days many different neighbors and friends dropped by to help out and to welcome the new baby. A few days later, Dr. Brown came for a visit. He wanted to check up on Rina and the baby, but he also made the visit as a friend.

In their conversation the doctor asked what they named the little boy so he could register the baby's birth legally when he returned to town. Rina proudly said that her son was named Jacob Samuel Rignez. The two names were from Sam and Rina's grandfather. Rina had great memories of her grandfather who came to his new country in the mid-1800s. He had been a religious leader and scholar in his younger days in central Europe.

In those early days of the development of the West, many people did not get to practice their original religion. Therefore, in many situations, because of a need for a religious rite to be expressed at a family celebration or special event, any local religious leader would be invited to officiate. Because of this need, a great feeling of community sharing developed in many of the early towns and villages. So, when Jacob was two months old, Rina and Sam made arrangements for the local Presbyterian pastor to say a few words over their little boy to welcome him officially to God's world of love and a future of a good life.

The local pastor was a fairly young man. He was a Scotchman through and through by the name of William MacTaggert. He claimed his denomination was of no particular calling and he was well accepted in the town and served his people well.

A small gathering attended the brief ceremony and everyone left the church with warm feelings for baby Jacob and his parents.

A short time later, Willow came to visit Rina and Jacob. After talking about their families for a while, Rina excused herself and when she came back, she had a very beautiful robe over her shoulder.

Rina gave the robe to Willow and said, "I saw this robe in town and just knew I should give this to you for being so helpful in bringing Jacob into the world and being very good to me. This is just a small way for me to say thank you, Willow."

Willow held the robe and stroked it in an appreciative way. She said, "Rina, I never expected this and there was no need for this. I know in my heart that you were thankful for my small way in helping you and Jacob. This is the first time in my life that a white person ever gave me anything. I will cherish this gift and this time forever. Please tell Samuel I said thank you."

Willow then added, "Rina, the only thank you I need is to know that someday you will pass on what I did to help you to some other woman in need of help. And I know you will do that, you have the good spirit from your heart to do such good things in life. We must always remember that this spirit must survive in this great country of ours or we will not continue as a whole people. Our great spirit shows us this every day in many ways."

Soon it was time for Willow to leave and return to her village and her family.

When Sam came home, Rina told him of her visit with Willow. Sam said, "I had a visit with her husband, Lone One. He and several of the men in his village are having a rattlesnake hunt in a few days. Evidently it has been dry weather for the rattlers and they are spreading out toward the village. A couple of children have been bitten, so they are going to thin them out. Then after the hunt they have planned a celebration. The main course will be rattlesnake!"

Rina said, "Yuck!" Sam added that he had been assured it would taste just like roast chicken.

Nine

As the days and months passed, Sam worked harder and harder and he slowly and consistently became quite prosperous. Several times he talked his more quiet partner, Cyrus Dutman, into gambling on a new business venture, and surprisingly, to both of them, the ventures were successful.

Sam seemed to have that magic touch in foreseeing possibilities of growth for the future. The area and local town were growing rapidly and Sam sensed the prosperity that could develop. Sam believed that if a man had the courage, backbone, and raw guts, he could become a huge success.

Sam told Rina, "I am trying to be a visionary and I believe somehow I am destined to be very successful here as we have grown together in what we are developing."

People in the area noticed that Sam was a good person to ask for advice. Because of the growth of the town and the area, the local small-time politicians faced many growing pains. It soon became evident that Sam and Cyrus Dutman, because of their success and general respect in the community, should be asked to serve in the local governing activities.

Cyrus told Sam that he felt honored to be considered, but he wanted nothing to do with politics. He was a strong individualist and he loved the open, western area because it gave him such freedom to make his own way. He was afraid of getting involved with anyone or anything that might change his style of living and his individual success. He then said, "My only exception to what I've just said is my friendship and relationship with you. You know by now how I feel about you, partner. Our area has grown and with our being a part of the growth, we have benefited. So, I believe we have a responsibility to pay back the good we have received."

"Sam," Cyrus continued, "I want you to represent the two of us in these local affairs. I will discuss all matters with you in private, but you can be the official voice in any of the meetings that come up. I have a feeling that you and I will end up being the real representatives of all the ranchers in our area. I believe this because of the conversations I have had with our neighbors."

Cyrus added, "Because of the expansive land we ranchers have, and the potential power and wealth it represents, I knew someday we would face this political picture. But, we must make sure that it benefits our operation. That will always be my priority. Yes, I have a selfish streak in me. If I didn't, I'd never survive out here."

After further discussion, the two agreed on how they would relate to the local political group.

Soon after this, Sam received an invitation to the National Cattleman's Convention in Chicago. One of the concerns of the more progressive ranchers was the improvement of their stock. Sam and Cyrus wanted their cattle to be bigger and stronger and to be able to handle the harsh weather conditions of the great western plains country.

Rina suggested that they should try to get their good friends the Weidmans and Favingers to join them in Chicago. Chicago was, after all, closer to them than Philadelphia.

The three families all finally agreed to meet in Chicago. Each of the three young families had sons who were close in age. The Weidmans' son was named David, and the Favingers' boy was Jerald. The trip on the train to Chicago with young two-year-olds was a challenge, but they made the most of it and had a great experience in the big city.

While in Chicago, Sam met a very interesting man about the same age as himself. Sam was walking through the hotel lobby on the way to a convention meeting when this muscular and husky looking young man stopped him. The man apologized for the interruption as he spoke with a heavy accent. "Please excuse myself for you—are you meeting with the cowboys people?"

Because of Sam's background, he felt for the man and knew what he was trying to say. He walked the man to a nearby chair and talked slowly to him. The man said he had trouble conversing with the hotel people and that they would not pay much attention to him.

Sam explained his background, where he was from, and that he was now a rancher and yes, he was at the convention. He told him he didn't have much time right then because of his meetings, but he would meet him later.

His new friend's name was Heiman Zobel, and he and his elderly father had a shoe store in north Chicago. The old man, Abel, had been a successful boot and shoemaker in southern Germany, but he became upset with living conditions in his country and made the decision to move to that land of opportunity, America the Beautiful.

It took them considerable time and hard work and they finally ended up in Chicago. After a time they started a small shoe repair shop in the Skokie area. Their plan was to keep saving money so they could send for the rest of their family which consisted of Abel's wife and two daughters.

The two new Americans were fascinated with their new country and found America to be as great as they dreamed it to be. They especially enjoyed all the stories of the development of the great West as well as the stories of cowboys, the ranchers and how the people lived and settled the rugged prairie country.

One day, Heimi (his Americanized name) began thinking of a few details of the cattle business. He wondered, with all the cattle shipped to the huge Chicago stockyards, what happened to all the hides after the slaughter process. Where the leather ended up was of interest to him because of his experience in the shoe business.

One weekend, Heimi had borrowed a friend's car to drive his father to southern Wisconsin to see the beautiful countryside in that area. On their way, they stopped for lunch in a small town of about a thousand people. Abel said the town, the people, and the countryside reminded him of Bavaria.

The people were having some type of celebration with dancing in the main street area. On a huge wood table there were several barrels of beer and wonderful bratwursts and sauerkraut to eat. The people were very friendly and hospitable.

The father and son sat down and had a nice visit with a group of people and they exchanged comments about the families as people do at such friendly events. After mentioning that they were in the shoe business, one of the local men suggested they should meet one of the local citizens who was trying to retire and sell his business.

Heimi's eyes lit up and he told his father it would be interesting to talk with the man about his business. So, they were led down the street to a table where the local cobbler was sitting with his wife and two married daughters.

They were introduced to Karl Burg, a jolly looking man with a flowing white beard. Heimi thought he could pass for the real Santa Claus!

After chatting and a few beers, the father and son asked about Karl's shoe business. Karl told the men how he had started out as a one-man operation. Today he had built it up to having ten men working for him. His main customers were people from the nearby towns and a few others from Chicago who would drop by on their annual vacation trips.

Karl told the father and son, "Let's go and visit my small shoe operation. It isn't far from here, just on the edge of town."

Karl drove the three men to the edge of town where his shop was located on the side of a small, beautiful meadow. The building was about sixty feet long and thirty feet wide. An attractive sign was over the front of the building which read "Karl's Shoes" and right below, "Our Shoes the Best."

Karl unlocked the front door which led into a small, neat office. "This," he said, "is where my wonderful wife keeps everything in order."

Karl then took his two guests on a tour of the shop. Abel and Heimi were very impressed with the shop and how well it was organized. The three men sat down and Karl brewed a pot of coffee. Karl gave a brief summary of his business. He said, "Each year my business grew—much to my surprise—but I am happy it went so well. I believe my success was in making high quality shoes and boots similar to the import products sold in the expensive men's stores. But," he said, "I'm getting tired and I don't want to work very hard anymore."

Karl added, "I feel lucky with the growth of my business because it was mostly by word of mouth and not by expensive advertising and promotion. I believe that someone with ambition and the ability to work hard could make the business thrive even more. I have been approached by a few stores in big cities for very large orders of shoes and boots—much larger than what I want to deal with."

The three men talked for a while and decided they would meet again the next weekend to further discuss the situation.

The next week Heimi got in touch with Sam because he wanted to ask him about cowhides. Heimi had a positive feeling about Sam. He believed he would be treated fairly and honestly by Sam.

After talking for a time, Heimi mentioned that he and his father were seriously thinking about investing in a small shoe/boot company. One of their big problems was the financing of the project. This made Sam pay closer attention to what Heimi was talking about and what would be involved in such a business transaction. Heimi's explanation of the deal sounded to Sam as if it had real possibilities.

Sam then mentioned to Heimi that he had a good contact for financing business ventures. He told Heimi that if he wanted Sam to approach his contact he would do so. Heimi, of course, said that he would like Sam to follow up on this idea.

Heimi and his father decided that they would invest in the shoe company if they could get financial assistance through Sam's contact.

Ten

Sam and Rina finished their visit with their friends, the Weidmans and the Favingers, and left for home the next day.

A week after returning to the ranch and settling down after their trip, Sam went into town to visit his friend, Lee Chinn. The two men met on a fairly regular basis. Lee was doing very well with his café. He was also considering to open two new cafes on the railroad line in the general area.

Sam told his friend about the man he had met in Chicago and his desire to take over a shoe and boot business, but that he was in need of financial help. Sam asked about Uncle Woo Chinn and how he was doing in Denver. Lee quickly brought Sam up to date on his Uncle Woo.

Evidently this man was close to being a genius in his business dealings. All his business investments were a huge success. He hired the right people and paid them well. He was a very private man and was always in the background, thus avoiding any publicity or notoriety.

Sam then asked Lee if he would arrange a meeting with his uncle so that he could explain the need for the Chicago man's financial assistance. Lee said he would follow up on this, but could not make any promises. Lee said his uncle had not been there for a visit for some time, so he would encourage him to make the trip.

Lee contacted his uncle and talked him into making the train trip to visit his nephew. Lee then met with Sam and they made their plans to meet with Uncle Woo the next week.

Sam always enjoyed socializing with the Woo family, so he told Lee they should meet at Sam's ranch and Rina would have an old-fashioned western barbecue for the occasion. Sam thought, after one of Rina's great meals at a beautiful outdoor setting, it would be a good way to talk business.

Lee met his uncle at the railroad depot and was in for a huge surprise. His uncle stepped off the Pullman car assisting a beautiful Chinese lady. The young lady was introduced as Uncle Woo's wife, Pearl. They had been married for over a month and she spoke very little English. The marriage had been arranged six months earlier with an old, wealthy, established family in San Francisco.

Uncle Woo's first wife had died six years earlier. Uncle Woo was in his early sixties and his new bride was nineteen. The pretty, young woman had long, shiny black hair that was arranged in a long pigtail to the bottom of her back. She was wearing a long silk dress that fell almost to her ankles. Lee thought she was an elegant looking woman.

The Woo family spent the evening in Lee's well-furnished apartment above the café. Sam and Rina stopped in for a visit and while the men chatted, Rina did her best to make young Pearl feel welcome.

After visiting for a time, Sam and Rina decided to head back to their ranch. The men had decided that they would meet early in the afternoon the next day.

Uncle Woo was up very early the next day before sunrise and told Lee that he wanted to see the beautiful sunrise at Sam's ranch. He'd heard that the sunrises and sunsets in this part of the great West were spectacular.

When Woo and Lee got to the ranch, they were told by Rina that Sam had gone to the south pasture to search for a few lost calves. Rina suggested they sit down in the front yard and watch the sunrise while she brought coffee and homemade bread out to them.

After an hour of visiting, Sam rode in and joined the group. Sam invited his friends for a short ride out on the range to show them his pride and joy—the ranch that he had built up from literally nothing.

Uncle Woo and Lee were fearful as they had never been on a horse in their lives. Sam told them not to worry as he had two old nags that never went faster than a walk, no matter how much you encouraged them.

Sam guided his friends on a slow tour of his ranch for several miles. They saw coyotes, gophers, pheasants, many other prairie birds, and also several snakes about which Sam told great stories.

After the ride, the two Chinese men were tired and had a few sore muscles from their long ride. They decided to return to town and get some rest. They would return in the middle of the afternoon for their meeting with Sam.

Willy made the trip into town to pick up the Chinns. Willy drove an elaborately decorated wagon, usually used at rodeos, which was pulled by two huge Belgian work horses. Willy told the guests that Sam was thinking of raising the Belgian horses as another small business venture. Willy wondered when Sam was going to slow down and stop getting into these extra business deals.

They arrived at the ranch house just in time to see and smell the delicious choice prime rib beef roasting on a large grill near the eating area that Rina and Sam had set up for the occasion.

Rina had two of Willow's teenaged daughters there to help with kitchen duties. The two girls could not keep from staring at Pearl as she was helped off the wagon. The only people they'd seen in their lifetimes were either Lakota Sioux or white people. They asked Rina while in the kitchen, "What kind of Indian is that woman—a Cherokee? She can't be an Arapaho, can she?"

Rina explained the situation. The girls said that their mother and father had told them stories of how the Great Spirit had created many other types of people on the other side of Mother Earth and that we should be friendly and appreciative of these people.

The dinner was delicious and a feeling of warm friendship was in the air. Rina escorted Pearl into the house and the men began their discussion of business financing.

The men sat around a glowing fire and discussed the shoeman in Wisconsin, as Uncle Woo referred to him and his business.

"Sam," Uncle Woo said, "you have done a good job of evaluating this business proposition. I believe your instincts are sound on this. Here is what I must do. I will go back east and personally meet these people and appraise things as I see it. Then I will make my decision."

Uncle Woo added, "Also, I need to make a trip to Chicago for another business encounter with some people I know. Remember what I am about to tell you and don't repeat these words to anyone. For a few years I have been doing some business with some Italian fellows who came to Denver. They have been very good to deal with, although a couple of my Chinese acquaintances are suspicious of them because of stories they have heard.

"These Italian men are very interesting. In some ways they are similar in words and actions as a few of my countrymen. For instance, they are very private people and they do not speak a word in front of other people in my presence. Also, the man in charge, Vito Rossi, has kept me a complete secret to his other partners in the East. I guess you could say we are silent partners.

"I mention this to you two young men because I know and trust you and I feel that someday you two will lead this small organization. This is enough for now. We will meet again soon and I am sure we will discuss some good news at that time."

With the end of the discussion the evening was over and the Chinns left for town.

The next day Uncle Woo and his wife were headed for home and within a week he departed on his trip East.

Upon arriving in Chicago, Uncle Woo met the next day with Heimi and Abel Zobel and they arranged for a trip to Wisconsin to look over the operation of the small shoe plant.

Uncle Woo spent the next two days with the men who knew the shoe business. He thoroughly looked over and studied all aspects of the small company.

After the two days were over, Uncle Woo told the Zobels that he would arrange financing for the purchase of the shoe plant. He told these men the same thing he had told his nephew and Sam earlier, "Don't tell anyone about our business arrangement. I will lay this all out soon for your acceptance, and we are now partners, but no one must know that. I will expect you, Heimi and Abel, to take over the operation formally in thirty days."

The next day the transaction was formalized and Uncle Woo departed for Chicago. Little did the Zobels know that their new shoe and boot venture would be successful in the next couple of years. Much of the success, of course, was due to their Chinese partner working quietly in the shadows of the business world.

Uncle Woo was invited to lunch by his Italian friend, Vito Rossi. Their first meeting was due to Vito finding out that Woo had a very intelligent grasp of the business development in Denver. Vito was looking for some factual information that he could get from Woo.

As they talked, the two men began to develop an appreciation for each other. Vito explained to Woo that he did business in a different way than several of his Italian friends. He said that he was trying continually to get these friends to follow his way of doing things—the honest and honorable way—the American way. Vito had earned his solid, honest reputation within the Italian community and was a popular leader in the city.

The two men developed a business agreement to help each other in new business prospects as they were discovered.

In the next few years they expanded their laundry businesses, Italian restaurants, shoe and boot stores and began the operation of real estate transactions throughout the Rocky Mountain states. The two men saw true potential in real estate in the western part of the country. The result was that in a short time, the two partners developed an organization equal to any blue chip company at that time.

Again, the two businessmen always remained in the background, never seeking any notoriety.

Eleven

It was a chilly, late October day and Sam got the wagon ready for the short ride into town for some of Rina's shopping needs. They bundled up little Jacob and headed for town.

They had just walked out of the local general store when an office clerk from the railroad depot jogged across the street and gestured to Sam. The young man told Sam a telegraph message had just arrived from the East and he thought it might be urgent.

Sam left his wife and quickly went to the railroad office to pick up the telegram. The message was from their good friend, Dan Favinger, but unfortunately was sad news. Dan's wife Lela had passed away a few days ago; more information would follow shortly.

A few days later, a lengthy letter arrived adding more sadness to the situation. Lela had come down with a bad cold and she thought she would be over it quickly. But the cold would not leave and it settled in her lungs. Then she was rushed to the hospital and diagnosed with pneumonia. Her endurance diminished quickly and she developed an extremely high fever. In two days Lela died.

The doctors informed Dan that Lela suffered what was actually diagnosed as a severe influenza virus that was spreading among the large cities of the East. They were worried that it might grow to epidemic levels.

Rina and Sam could not make arrangements in time to travel East to attend Lela's funeral service. They sent a telegram to Dan expressing their sorrow of his great loss and said they would plan a visit in the near future.

Sam carved a simple wooden marker and engraved their friend Lela's name to it and placed it on the edge of their ranch house yard. Simply carved on the wooden marker's surface were the words, "We will remember you forever." Rina placed wildflowers around the marker whenever they were in bloom.

Twelve

Sam and Rina's ranch flourished for the next year and their income increased. They were two generous people and whenever possible they helped those who were in need of assistance. Sam and Rina had their life going in the right direction. They had found true happiness in their lifestyle and young Jacob was a total joy to them.

Springtime came early that year and after harsh, late and harsh winter weather, people welcomed the spring weather scenery.

But, soon another tragedy came to Sam and Rina. A telegram was delivered with more sad news from Philadelphia. Mr. Favinger, Dan's father, sent a wire telling of the passing away of his son Daniel. And like the last time, a letter came a few days later from Mr. Favinger telling more of his son's unfortunate death. Dan was riding a street car in downtown Philadelphia during the busy noontime rush hour. As he positioned himself to jump off of the car, it made a sudden jerking motion and Dan lost his footing and fell to his death on the cobblestone street

Sadly, in one year, young Jerald had lost both of his loving parents.

Sam and Rina quickly made arrangements to make the trip East to be with the grieving family. They left their trusty ranch foreman, Willy, in charge of the operations in their absence.

The young family left early one morning to make the long trip to their old hometown known as the city of Brotherly Love. During their travel young Jacob was very adventurous and his parents had to watch him closely as he ran up and down the passenger cars.

On the last day of travel Rina noticed that Jacob was not hungry at all and did not seem to have much energy. By that evening Jacob was running a fever and was quite ill.

The conductor noticed their concern and did what he could to help out. He mentioned that many people were complaining of the influenza sickness that had increased during that time of year. He strongly suggested that upon their arrival in Philadelphia they get the child to a doctor right away.

That evening, when the train pulled into the large Philadelphia train station, Ira and Sarah Weidman were there to meet them and they went directly to the Weidmans' home.

By this time Jacob was extremely ill. Sam and Rina immediately took their son to their friends' family doctor, who was located in the neighborhood.

After examining Jacob, the doctor said he was severely infected with influenza which was breaking out all over the city. The doctor said the child must go to the hospital right away and he personally drove the family there.

Being a friend of the Weidmans, the doctor used his influence to get Jacob admitted to the overcrowded hospital. Jacob was immediately put in a room where they administered oxygen to him. The doctor said, "We will see how he is in the morning, but now we must all pray for Jacob to win this battle he is facing."

This outbreak of influenza seemed to attack younger ones as severely as the older people. Weakening of the lungs and high fevers seemed to be the downfall of most victims.

Sam and Rina stayed close by Jacob's bedside the whole night praying continually for their son's recovery. But unfortunately, Jacob's fever rose to an unrelenting pitch and his young body suffered immensely. His breathing by early morning was almost nonexistent.

As the sun rose over the city of Brotherly Love, young Jacob Rignez's body lost its battle of pain and suffering.

Sam and Rina were left with broken hearts over the death of their child. Added to the heartbreak was the fact that Rina found out a few months earlier in an examination by Dr. Brown that she would be unable to bear any more children.

Soon after the burial of young Jacob, Rina said to Sam, "With all of our misery over our losses, everyone seems to have forgotten Dan and Lela's young son, Jerald. We have all overlooked that the boy is now an orphan."

Rina added, "I have thought this through, and I feel we should discuss this with Mr. Favinger. I know he is more than eighty years old and it would be very difficult for him to take care of his grandson. The other family members are not in a position to do much better.

"I believe it is God's will that Jerald should be with us. I truly believe this is a gift from the Lord and meant to be an act of love to mend our hearts and souls as well as providing a future for the young boy."

Rina continued, "Loneliness is a horrible sadness. Too much loneliness within a person can crush a person's spirit. Sam, we cannot let this happen to this boy. We are being given a great purpose in life to tend to; we must do this. In our time together, you have told me many stories of your hardships and rough experiences in your travels to this country, and in those times you endured terrible loneliness. So, let's please do this for Jerald. I know we will never regret it."

Sam agreed with Rina and they decided to talk to other family members.

When they met with the family, one of Dan and Lela's cousins said that he was worried that if word got to the authorities of the State Orphan's Agency, that they might step in and take over Jerald's life and place him in an orphanage. It was a viable concern because this sort of thing happened to many orphans—especially those of immigrant parents. Politicians and city officials thought it best to have these homeless waifs in orphanages rather than having them running loose on the streets.

Finally, Sam stood up and said, "You have all given your opinions about Jerald's future and I appreciate that but we are talking about this boy's life! You all know Rina and me. You have shown your respect and love to us. Rina and I would like to take Jerald into our home and raise him as our son. We can leave here quickly and quietly with Jerald and if we say nothing of this meeting to anyone, believe me nothing will happen. Jerald will be welcomed into a new and loving home."

The Favinger family saw Sam and Rina's sincerity and humbleness and everyone agreed that Jerald would be well-taken care of, and that the best solution was for him to be with Sam and Rina.

Thirteen

ina did a wonderful bit of storytelling to her new son to prepare him for the long train trip ahead which she emphasized as a fun, exciting adventure.

One day on the train, Sam told Jerald a story about Jacob. He made it a very colorful and enjoyable story for his new son. He told Jerald, "It's a nice name for a boy and maybe you would like to be called Jacob." The boy, who was just two years old, liked the idea.

Rina was still grieving the loss of their son Jacob but agreed with Sam that they would adopt Jerald and give him the name of Jacob Rignez.

Somehow the two parents found it easier to refer to their new son as Jake and from that time on he answered to either Jake or Jacob. The past was gone and the boy stepped into a new life.

Finally, the westbound train reached its destination on a late afternoon. Willy was there to meet them and give them a happy welcome home and a special western greeting to Jake. They loaded up the wagon and headed out across the prairie. The family was very tired from their trip and happy to finally be home.

Young Jake was quite excited with the surrounding prairie country. Willy kept telling the boy great stories about the area to create more interest in their local lifestyle. Rina and Sam appreciated this and felt that Willy's friendliness would help Jake feel more at home.

Willy also mentioned that two of their favorite mares had just had beautiful colts—one a male, the other a female. Sam said, "Jake, which pony you would like for your own?"

With that comment the youngster was filled with joy and happiness. What a welcome home gift this was!

Sam and Rina shared the story about Jake's background with just their closest friends. Jake grew up knowing Sam and Rina as his only parents.

As summer came that year, it developed into a hot one. Many times Sam would take Jake to their large watering tank back by the main barn and take a refreshing dip to cool off.

Over the summer and into the fall, Jake learned the exciting lifestyle of ranch kids. He became fascinated with all the different things there were to do. He followed his father around every day like a lost puppy, except for the times when there could be some danger involved. For instance, when Willy and Sam put six-shooters on their hips, they would not let Jake come near.

Sam and Rina explained to the boy that once in a while they had to hunt down some unwanted varmints that could become serious problems on the ranch. This type of experience taught the boy about firearms and overall gun safety.

As Jake learned from Sam and witnessed all of the man's skills from day to day, he knew his father must be a really great man and wondered how he knew so much.

Rina was a fine teacher as well as a very good mother. It was amazing how much she taught Jake before he went to school. At the boy's young age, Rina taught him in bits and pieces about math, writing, and reading.

Just as important to Sam and Rina was the development of Jake's character traits and his relationships with people. Through the years Jake would become close friends of Lakota Sioux, Mexicans, Chinese, blacks, and all other Americans. This diversity helped prepare Jake for the many obstacles he would face in his future years.

As time went by, Sam and Rina noticed how the West and their area in particular was continuing to grow. The railroad had tremendous growth and was the main transportation for all types of people—farmers, homesteaders, merchants, lawyers, gamblers—all types of people basically looking for the same thing, a decent start and future in the great West which offered many opportunities.

Sam and Rina's main business continued to be the cattle industry. As their cattle herd continued to grow, they purchased more and more range land with the cooperation of their friend, Cyrus Dutman.

Sam was surprised at how well the Zobel father-son shoe business had progressed in Wisconsin. Heimi, the son, was very successful in developing new business for the small company. But, the way they were growing, they would no longer be a small operation. Heimi had managed to make contact with some military and government people to begin making shoes and boots for the military. It was difficult dealing with bureaucrats in the government, but Heimi was very persistent and finally won a small contract to make some boots and shoes for the army.

This development added more work, of course, and an extra work shift had to be added to the plant. A request also came from a high-class men's store for some exotic western styles and cowboy boots such as snake skin and other animal hides.

The Zobels immediately contacted Sam to find out what he knew about different skins and hides for boots. Sam knew right away, and saw the possibilities for getting the materials. He and Rina rode their wagon across the prairie for a social visit with the Tall Tree family near Dutmans' ranch.

Although they were going mainly for a social visit, Sam was sure that Lone Tall Tree would have good advice about snake skins and animal hides.

While Rina and Willow visited and talked about their children, Sam talked with Lone Tall Tree, who went by Lone, about skins and hides for Sam's friends in the shoe business.

Sam explained the proposal to Lone and made him aware that if he and his people assisted in providing skins and hides it could be a profitable situation for them.

Then Lone asked, "Sam, what kind of people are these men? Are they like you? In our conversation you said they were originally from Germany. I know little of people like that. I've heard that people over there—where you came from—are great warriors, just like the Lakota Sioux were some years ago. Are these men warriors?"

Lone added, "Sam, I've never been to a big city like you have. Many of my people have not been to a big city. If I am to do business with these men, I would like to know more about them."

Sam told his friend, "The shoe men were not soldiers or warriors. They were businessmen and very hard workers. They came to America to gain freedom and a better way of life. In Europe, certain people were restricted in their particular lifestyle and personal beliefs. Lone, I am sure that you would get to like Abel and Heimi Zobel."

Sam suggested they get one or both of the Zobel men to come visit so they could work out a deal. This would give Lone a chance to meet them and they could speak easier about specifics.

Lone agreed to this idea and Sam made contact with the Zobels and sold them on the idea of a visit. Surprisingly, both the father and the son decided to make the trip. The two men said they wanted to know more about the West.

A few days later, the Zobels arrived at the train depot. The two men were not sure what to expect of their trip or of the prairie town they were visiting, but they were impressed with what they saw.

The wide-open space was something to behold, especially after spending most of their lives in big cities. The men hopped in Sam's wagon and had a leisurely ride out to Sam's ranch.

The next day they all rode out to visit the Tall Tree family. Late that afternoon Willow prepared a fine grilled dinner of grouse and pheasants. The evening was spent around a campfire trading stories about each other's families; it was a huge success.

The following day, Lone gave the visitors a tour of the area, showing them the spots that were best for hunting and trapping various snakes and animals. Lone took them on the tour to show what was involved, especially the fact that there was some danger involved in getting and handling the snakes.

The Zobels wanted to see some hides and skins and Lone had some on hand. The tribal people occasionally used these to make some traditional Sioux clothes and moccasins. These were mostly for spiritual ceremonial gatherings.

The men finally sat down and discussed the details of their business arrangement. Sam acted as the mediator and was very instrumental in finalizing the deal. They reached an agreement selling the hides and skins and the first shipment was scheduled to be delivered in two weeks.

At the end of the meeting all of the men shook hands and mentioned how they looked forward to doing business with each other.

At this time, almost all shoe companies used strictly cowhides for shoes and boots so the Zobels were really starting a new trend in the business. Their customers were mainly stores that catered to people looking for something different, no matter what the expense. These customers were mostly affluent people in larger cities.

The Zobels were aware of this and decided to make high quality shoes and boots and charge a top price for their products. This new part of the business became an immediate success. It also became an economic success for the people in Lone Tall Tree's village out in the west prairie country.

Fourteen

Sam was again asked to attend a meeting of the cattlemen's organization in Chicago the following spring. Sam had been appointed as a representative of the ranchers in his western plains area. Sam really did not want to go, but decided he had a responsibility to attend.

Sam asked his Chinese friend, Lee Chinn, to make the trip with him as he knew Lee also had business to attend to in the city. The two men from the West were met at the station by their mutual friend, Vito Rossi.

The next day Vito told his two friends about a family problem he was having and asked for their advice. "My sister Marie is a widow. Her husband was killed in an Italian gang-style shootout a couple of years ago. She has been well-taken care of financially, but her main problem is raising her children. She has two beautiful daughters less than seven years old, but her problem is with her fourteen-year-old son, Anthony.

"At the loss of my brother-in-law, I did what I could to help my sister and be a father figure to young Tony. The boy loved his father dearly, and his death drastically changed Anthony. Marie seems to have lost all control over her son, and I do not know how to handle the boy. It seems all my effort to help the boy have failed.

"At fourteen Tony is a good-sized young man at about five feet ten inches tall, and one hundred sixty pounds. He is blessed with a lot of natural strength. He enjoys sports at school and shows a lot of promise as a football player.

"Tony had been a good-natured lad and was always happy. But, he has changed. At school he gets into fights every day, and he appears to be miserable. The school principal told his mother that if he does not change his behavior, he will be expelled.

"Recently, I tried a different approach with the boy. Because of his physical abilities and interest in sports, I thought of introducing the boy to boxing. I knew a Greek man who managed a boxing gym on Chicago's south side, and he decided to check out the gym. The man, Nick Sopolos, has the reputation of being fair and honest with all the amateur and professional boxers that work out at his gym.

"The gym is on the second floor of an old, abandoned factory building. It isn't fancy, but it is roomy and the rent is cheap. I told Nick the sad story about my sister's son and that I was seeking help and was at my wit's end with the problem.

"Nick responded by saying that he could understand my frustration. He mentioned that in his rough and tough business he dealt with all kinds of young men—white, black, Mexican, Indian and many former Europeans. He treated them all the same and in many cases ended up being almost a family member to them."

Vito added, "Nick said that he would meet with the boy and explain the ground rules of the gym operation, and he would work with him for two weeks on a trial basis. But the boy would have to follow the rules.

"So, Tony met with Nick. They talked about the program and Tony agreed to give it a try. At first Nick had to be very strict with Tony. Tony wanted to do things his way—just jump in the ring and slug it out with some guy. But on those first days Nick had the boy work on the basics of being a boxer, not a thug or a bully. Nick had him do road work, stretching exercises, shadow boxing, hitting the speed bag and the heavy bag. At the end of these workouts the boy was worn out.

"On the third day, Nick put Tony in the ring for some sparring. Nick set up Tony's match with a young black man known as Spider. His name came from the man's appearance—very long legs and arms. Nick confided in Spider about Tony's background, and told Spider he was to carry or take it easy on Tony for the three rounds of boxing. Spider was a natural one hundred sixty pounder and a top contender in Chicago's middleweight division.

"Nick counseled Tony in his warmup session as to how he should approach his opponent. But once in the ring, Tony ignored—or forgot—what Nick had advised him to do. As the bell rang for the match to start, Tony rushed straight across the ring like a wild bull. Spider deftly took a step to the side and Tony went flying through the ropes and landed on his hands and knees on the gym floor.

"Nick and Spider quickly rushed to the boy's side to see if he was okay. Tony was mad and humiliated. The two men helped the boy to his feet and the three of them sat down in the ring.

"Nick said, 'We are going to walk through a round of boxing to explain what you have to do to win the round'."

"And that is what Nick did with the boy. Nick was very calm and easy in his lecture about boxing. Somehow he got through to this young bull of a man. Nick had Tony and Spider start the match over and Spider controlled the remaining rounds. Even though Tony was not the winner, he showed promise as a boxer. Tony's real asset as an athlete is his overall physical strength."

Vito said "The boxing thing is working out so far but that I have one more idea to try on Tony if the boxing routine does not work out. My idea would be to move the boy out to a ranch out West and involve him in a whole new way of living. I think that may be the change that would shape up Tony mentally and emotionally.

Vito asked, "Sam, what is your opinion on this idea? Would it be difficult to find a place for the boy out west?"

Sam replied, "There is a big difference in the living style out West. It is far different out there than in the city of Chicago, but there are many advantages."

Sam then told some brief stories of men who went west at a young age and became very successful. In each of those cases he pointed out that these men had a few things in common—they were extremely hard workers, had a desire to succeed, and have a great deal of confidence themselves.

Sam explained that there was always a need for good hard workers on the ranches and large farms out in the west prairie country. Tony's success would depend on Tony and his desire to help himself. Nothing would be given freely to him. Sam promised Vito that if the boy headed west, Sam would have a job lined up for him.

The three men finished their evening together and made plans to have another visit in the near future. Vito had high hopes of getting young Tony back to a normal lifestyle.

The next day Sam and Lee finished their business in Chicago and headed back to their home in the West.

Fifteen

or the next three years Tony did very well. Then one day Tony got into a fight at school. He was beating up his opponent quite badly when a teacher attempted to break up the fight. Tony quickly turned his aggression on the teacher. With two fast punches to the man's head, the teacher was dropped to the floor in a heap. The teacher suffered a broken nose and a dislocated jaw.

It took three other men to subdue Tony. A policeman came to the school and escorted Tony to the juvenile section of the police department.

The next week Tony had to appear in court. His mother and Vito went with the boy. The parents of the other boy wanted to press charges against Tony, but Vito's lawyer persuaded the judge to have the complaint dropped and instead give a stern lecture to both boys. The judge had a more serious plan for Tony due to the attack of the teacher.

After reviewing Tony's background and problems, the judge decided to give the boy some options. At this time Tony was seventeen years old and the judge thought the young man should be in a situation where he would receive a continuous amount of supervision. The judge gave Tony the option of joining a national CCC work program, which had been introduced in the 1930s, or enlist in the army for the minimum enlistment period of two years.

Surprisingly, Tony made the decision to enlist in the army. The judge warned Tony he would have to go by the rules of the military or he could be in some serious trouble. The boy was expected to enlist within sixty days at which time he would be close to eighteen years old.

Soon after things were settled with Tony, Vito wrote to Sam and told him what had happened. Vito said that hopefully the young man would shape up. Vito promised to keep Sam up-to-date on Tony.

By this time, Rina and Sam decided to buy a house in town because their many activities were requiring more and more of their time there. Also, Jake was just starting high school. The move into town was convenient for them, but they still planned to spend time at the ranch. Jake had grown to be quite the young man and a big help to his father on the ranch.

The house in town was very comfortable for the family. Sam, with suggestions from Rina, made improvements to the house. Three extra rooms were added to the house and the kitchen doubled in size.

Sam also took advantage of their very large lot and built a small barn and pen on the back property. Sam enjoyed the open space of their new home in town and would always have a couple of horses in the barnyard. As Rina would always say, "Sam, you are just a cowboy at heart."

Moving into town was also a plus for Jake. Living on the ranch, he was limited in socializing with his friends. Now, as school was about to start, he would see his pals every day.

Jake heard about preseason football practices which were about to start. He asked his parents for permission to sign up for the sport and Sam and Rina encouraged him to join the program.

Jake, now fourteen years old, had grown to a good sized young man. Having done hard work at the ranch, he became very strong and sturdy.

The first football practice started on a very hot August afternoon. Most of that first week was spent on conditioning and basic fundamentals of the coach's offensive system. The football coach soon found out that Jake had sure and quick feet.

There were more than one hundred boys out for the football team. By the end of the first week, twenty-five freshmen were assigned to the all-freshman squad. Two freshmen boys, Jake and his new pal Mitz, were picked to be on the varsity squad. This was quite an accomplishment for the two freshmen.

When the three varsity coaches were asked about the two making the varsity squad, the coaches said it was because the two boys were very tough mentally and physically and seemed to have natural instincts for the game.

Mitz was a real scrapper and hard to knock off his feet and the coaches planned to have him play guard. Meanwhile, Jake was scheduled to play blocking back in the coaches single wing formation. The two boys, because of their inexperience, probably would not start any games, but would gain some valuable experience their first year.

That was an interesting year for the Rignez family. Jake was well adjusted to living in town by now and participated in different sports and school activities. The boy thoroughly enjoyed all his new friends and experiences while sharing his time between the town and the ranch.

Sixteen

One hot summer day after football practice, the coach asked Jake and Mitz to meet with him in his office.

Jake said to Mitz, "What have we done now?"

The coach sat the boys down near his desk and closed the office door—which seemed to be an odd thing to do. The two ball players had never seen the coach close his office door.

The coach said, "I need your help. We've had a new family move into town. Their last name is Fonder. The father's name is Bill Fonder and he's been transferred here by the railroad people. Bill and his wife Mary have three children—John, Bill, and daughter Lisa. Bill, the father is known as a hard worker and very fine person with a strong Baptist church background and as a lay minister."

At this point the two boys were somewhat confused. Where was coach going with this?

The coach felt sure these two would follow up on this favor to him. Mr. Fondor's job was to be the supervisor of the many dining car employees who would be going through the local town.

"From what I've told you I'm sure you understand that this is a black family. This means you'll have a new teammate. I want you two to help him get to know some of the other players."

The coach said they would meet their new team member the next day.

The coach had met the father and son the previous day and was very impressed with them.

Mr. Fonder had given the coach an introductory letter from the young man's last coach.

The father and son soon left and the coach sat down to read the letter. The letter described the new player in glowing terms—six foot two and 190 pounds and ran the 100 in 10.2 seconds, plus he had great desire and could hit a ton! The coach finished the letter. He told himself that he hoped the new player could deliver on the field and not just on this paper.

The previous coach also said near the end of the letter that he was familiar with the level of football in the local town and that if he played his new player right the new team could probably win the area football championship. What a great idea—to see his players become champs.

Because of the growth of the railroad and the local town, there was also a growth of black employer and as a result small (Black Only) small hotel and restaurant developed.

Joe Smith was the key investor in this business venture. With the additional number of employees passing through town, they had the need for sleeping rooms, a place to eat, and recreation of some type.

The recreation that developed was card playing—poker became the big attraction. Social card games were played, but many serious poker players attended.

Unfortunately once in a while some undesirable players dropped in. Some were worse, downright dangerous if they went into a bad losing streak.

Joe Smith met and hired a black man from this railroad to manage the hotel operation. The name he went by was Box Car. One look at him and you would know how he got his name. He was huge! He was six foot three and weighed in at 275 pounds. He was polite and calm, but capable of violently exploding. Before getting into railroad food service he worked in Chicago's tough south side in various cafes and hotels. So, he knew his business.

Joe had set up a special room in the back of the building for the recreation/poker activities so the entry was controlled at the restaurant area. Joe had the place well organized and covered and it appeared that it would be a small gold mine.

John Founder approached Joe Smith about a part time job at the Hotel/Restaurant. Joe of course had heard of John and what a fine young man he was. Joe hired the young man to do menial work—washing dishes and serving food. He was paid $1.50 an hour and worked evenings on Saturday and Sunday.

On an extremely busy Saturday night a very serious poker game developed.

At what Box Car called the star table, there were eight players. Two of the men had all the markings of big city card sharks—dangerous, smart and vicious when upset. Box Car paid special attention to them and called his boss to have the sheriff drop by for a short, friendly visit as a precaution.

Just what they had worried about happened. One of the town's regular players caught one of the sharks cheating and with a couple thousand dollars cash on the table all hell broke loose. Box Car jumped right in to end the violence and at that same instance young John Founder walked in from the kitchen with a large tray of sandwiches. He, by a bad stroke of luck, walked right into one of the sharks swinging a sharp pointed bottle opener. With a lot of force, the opener struck John across his stomach before he knew what was happening.

Wearing a light summer tee shirt, nothing could stop this horrible weapon from tearing John wide open.

Two police officers arrived and raced the young man to the hospital. John, a fine addition to the community was pronounced dead thirty minutes later at 17 years of age.

Many people mourned at John's funeral. Many tears were shed over the terrible loss of this young man.

The murderer of John was locked up in tight security. The town had very strong feelings about this type of crime and there still some believers of old-fashioned justice.

A meeting was set up by a few of these old timers to see that justice was done properly. Word got out about the meeting to the sheriff and he immediately got in touch with Sam. Sam Rignez was respected by all in town and the sheriff talked him into going to the meeting and calming down the possible lynch mob.

Sam was not directly invited to the meeting but with his strong ways of handling himself he got into the meeting.

After arguing for a few hours the situation cooled down and the real hot heads finally agreed to do nothing in a violent nature.

Before sunrise the next morning, law enforcement officers transported the mean-tempered shark securely chained and gagged out of town in a railroad baggage car. He was taken to a city in the east to face trial.

True to the form of western justice the man was tried and sentenced to the death penalty.

Seventeen

By the 1930s, which were better known as the Dirty Thirties, most people were beginning to improve their lives economically following the Great Depression.

Some people did not pay much attention to worldwide news and political events during those days. But, through the news media, there was more and more bad news about the horror stories of the German Nazi war machine invading other European countries. Some predicted war. Others paid no attention. Eventually war did come and the lives of many were changed forever.

Just after the start of World War II in 1941, the United States government decided to develop additional paratrooper training facilities on the outskirts of the local prairie town. This was done basically because of the vast wide-open countryside which was ideal for the training of airborne troopers.

This development, which should bring thousands of troopers and civilian staff, would change the town in a big way, to say the least. After the struggle of the thirties, the economy received a healthy boost due to the new jobs and new dollars coming to town. Spirits rose higher and higher. This type of wartime growth happened in many communities all over the country.

The western prairie town became a real boom town. More money in town meant more spending, and a lot of money was spent wildly.

Soon after, the war was in full swing and the Selective Service Act went into effect, both of which caused a shortage of men to fill many jobs. Young men, such as Jake, were encouraged to secure some of the more basic and unskilled jobs at the paratrooper base.

Sam thought Jake should get a job at the base. He thought it would be a good experience for his son and he would be doing something for the war effort.

So, Jake and a couple of his pals got summer jobs with the maintenance department at the paratrooper base. They worked with a few local men and a few soldiers doing time in the Military Police's garrison for various military infractions. The young men's jobs were basic pick and shovel labor jobs.

In addition to learning about taking on a grown man's workload, these young men learned more about the "facts of life." They found out there was more to a job than picking up a paycheck once a week; in working for the military, they had to have discipline and show they were responsible.

Early one summer day, Jake and his friend Mitz were assigned to barrack's duty. The day was extremely hot and the department foreman put them to work removing storm windows from the window frames. One worker would hold the main inner window and his partner would pull the storm window and lean it against the wall.

A tough unforeseen problem arose immediately. The two other young men on the opposite side, John and Ray, literally, and for some time, had a deep hatred against Mitz. These young men were all about the same size, but John was known as one tough hombre and had the reputation of being the town's biggest bully. In addition, he had a mean and viscous streak in him.

After the foreman left the facility, John started a viscous tirade against Mitz. All his comments were mean anti-Semitic remarks which touched Mitz to his very core as a young Jewish man.

The two friends tried to ignore the insults, but the two bullies continued their verbal assault. After a couple of minutes Jake had heard enough abuse and told the two wise guys to shut up.

That was all John wanted to hear—any excuse to launch an attack on an unsuspecting enemy. He waited for the minute when Jake and his buddy both had a window in their hands and rushed over and smashed the windows over Jake's head. Then the two of them attacked Mitz in a viscous fury. Jake, with the window frame down over his head and jagged pieces of glass raked over his head and face, was in an awkward position to be of any help to his friend.

Jake's face and head were a bloody mess and his eyes were filled with blood and his nose was bent and bloody. He had to struggle to get the window frame off and in doing so the splinters of broken glass cut his hands.

Meanwhile, Mitz was having a rough struggle of his own. Fighting two tough bullies at a time was a rough assignment.

Fortunately, a sergeant heard the commotion and terrible verbal abuse coming from the barracks and ran inside and broke up the disturbance. He immediately had a corporal who was assisting him contact the base hospital and ambulance service. The major in charge of the hospital section immediately had John and Ray fired because of the brutal attack. He informed the two troublemakers that because they were civilians, a full report of the incident would be turned over to the local police department.

Jake was then taken to the base hospital where he was stitched up. He was given a complete examination before his discharge. A doctor gave him a ride home and told him to take off a couple of days from work. He also had to explain to Sam and Rina how he and Mitz became involved in this unfortunate experience. After hearing the story of the abuse directed at Mitz, Sam and Rina were proud of him for standing up for his friend.

Mitz ended up in bad shape and remained in the base hospital overnight for further observation. Mitz had experienced a few other anti-Semitic encounters, but nothing as severe as this.

Eighteen

The years went by and Sam had become a very contented man. He was a successful rancher whose most enjoyable cowboy activity was working with his horses. Sam was a natural in working with all animals, but he had a special feeling for horses. Due to this interest, he always had a couple of his favorite horses in a pen behind the house in town.

Sam was becoming known as an expert in the area because of his success in breaking and training horses. Soon he was approached by all types of people to train and break their horses. This, at first a hobby in his spare time, grew and grew and became somewhat of a problem in taking too much of his time.

West of town, about twenty-five miles, there was a small valley. The valley was about ten miles long and quite a beautiful countryside to admire. It was also a natural haven for wild horses. Hardly any white men knew of this isolated valley. Sam learned of the valley through Lone Tall Tree. Lone told Sam that his family had used the valley for more than a hundred years.

Based on his need for horses, Sam would go to the valley and collect a few at a time. This could be wild, rough work for him and his cowboys. First they would pick the best of the herd, from ten to twelve mustangs—then catch the horses and take them back to the ranch corral.

On his first jaunt to the valley, young Jake proved to be an excellent horseman. Sam had taught the young man well, and was very proud of him in the way he carried his workload.

The word spread far and wide about Sam who could do so much in the training of horses. Most of his expertise was centered on ranch horses. They had to be strong, quick, and have great heart—as Sam would say.

One experience that Sam never forgot, happened just months before the start of World War II and related to horses. On a bright summer day, an army vehicle drove up to the ranch house. A very large, handsome man in full cavalry uniform with highly polished boots, asked for Sam.

After eyeballing each other and chatting for a time, they both felt inwardly that they could become friends for a long time. Soon the cavalry officer made his point for the visit. He said, "I am the commanding officer in charge of Fort Robinson to the north. I am very aware of your success in working with the horses. I have the authority to contract with you for the purchase of horses each year for our United States Cavalry unit."

Sam brought Willy, his ranch foreman, into the discussion at this point. The officer was impressed with the cowboy and his evident ability for horse training and knowledge of western mustangs. After much discussion and negotiation, a deal was made.

As the friendly army man was about to depart, he stopped and said, "I am not sure if you men are aware, but we might be at a point in time where wars and battles will be fought without a Cavalry or horses in any way. The main military force in the future will be the tank and other mechanized vehicles. Mark my words gentlemen, sooner than I would ever want we could be involved in a large, horrible war."

So the storm clouds continued and the world waited for an unbelievable horror to begin.

Nineteen

am was always an early riser. He truly loved their house in town and admired Rina's touch in continuing to improve the comforts of their home. Each morning Sam would leisurely stroll around the house and yard admiring everything.

Early this particular fall morning he heard a different, unfamiliar sound coming from the back barn. He wondered what it could be—possibly a small animal? Sam at this time wore his six-shooter holstered on his hip. He quietly circled the barn hoping to surprise the varmint and chase it away without any harm to anyone.

He squeezed through a broken board in the wall by the horse stall and crept over to where the light rustling sound was coming from. What a surprise! A young lad, maybe sixteen years old with olive skin and jet black hair, was sitting in the stall doing something with a pair of moccasins.

Sam had his six-shooter pointed at the young man, which not only surprised him, but scared him to death. The young man jumped and rolled away from this dangerous looking creature.

Sam holstered his gun and grabbed the stranger. Sam took a good grip on the young man's thick hair and forced him to the floor. With some anger in his voice he bellowed, "What in the hell are you doing here?"

The young man said, "I needed a place to rest. I was afraid to go into town. I have been told that I should stay away from white people and this was handy to get into as I was trying to walk past your town. I'm just passing through. I'm trying to work my way to Oklahoma where I have relatives. I meant no harm to you. I was just so tired."

Sam asked where he was from. He replied, "I am from the Pine Ridge area. Life has been miserable there. I'm the oldest of five children and my stepfather sent me away. He said it was time to become a man and learn to feed and clothe myself. From my few experiences in life I believe the old ways of living by my people are not going to help us survive in the future."

Sam, a kindhearted man, decided to be a little soft in dealing with the boy. The raggedy moccasins were splitting apart and the boy's feet were cut and bleeding in several spots. Sam had the boy follow him to the kitchen at the back of his house.

Rina was up by this time and had the coffeepot going. She said good morning to the young fellow and left the kitchen.

Sam went to his bedroom and brought out a pair of his older, beat-up boots and handed them to the youngster saying, "Wear these until your feet heal and you fix your moccasins. You can temporarily sleep in the loft of the barn. Whatever you receive here isn't free, you will work for everything you receive. Then when you are ready you can hit the trail for Oklahoma."

The next day Sam introduced the young man to Rina and Jake. He was very polite and said very little. Sam told Jake to show the boy around the ranch.

Sam explained the situation to Willy and told him to work the boy hard and see what he was made of. So, for the next week the youngster did everything Sam and Willy told him to do with a positive, happy spirit. After a couple of days, Sam sat down with the boy and asked, "I need to know what to call you. I can't just keep yelling 'hey you!'"

The boy replied, "My father named me Line Walker. He said I would be special and that someday I would walk all the lines and trails leading my tribe to the end of the earth when necessary in search of peace and prosperity. Unfortunately, times have been hard for my people and so far, I have not been a good leader. My father died a tragic death as a young man and won't know how I ended up in this lifetime."

Sam said, "Well young man, I'll just call you Line to keep things simple and you can call me Sam like most people do."

Days passed and soon the two developed a close relationship. Line was a couple of years older than Jake and they became very close friends. Over the years they would become more like brothers.

Soon, as Line became more accepted as a regular ranch hand, he gave up his plan to head for Oklahoma. One day Sam asked the young man about going to Oklahoma and Line said, "I would like to stay on and work for you if you could fit me into the permanent ranch crew."

Sam said, "It's a deal!"

Over the period of a few years, Line grew in many ways. He was sensible, had a positive attitude, and developed a fierce loyalty to Sam and Rina. He thought of Sam as a superman. Due to the strenuous physical labor on the ranch, he developed a good-sized muscular body similar to Sam in structure.

Sam, for some unknown reason, started calling his young friend Lane. This name caught on and soon all the neighbors and friends were calling him Lane. By this time, Lane had developed in another way—he grew to be an exceptionally handsome man and the women and girls certainly noticed this.

One day Cyrus and Anna Dutman's youngest daughter was getting married and after the ceremony there was a beautiful party at the Dutman's ranch.

At the party Lane noticed a very pretty, young woman with long auburn hair and large, hazel eyes. After observing the great-looking woman, he just knew he had to meet her right away. He went to Rina and asked for an introduction to the lady—and she certainly was a lady as Lane found out. Her name was Maria Cardoza, the daughter of Juan and Cara Cardoza. Juan was the chief gandy dancer for the railroad and ran a hard-driving crew of men for the railroad.

The Cardozas were the parents of four children and Maria was the oldest. After high school Maria went east for some training to become a nurse. When she returned to her hometown, she immediately secured a position at the local hospital. She soon became a very accomplished nurse and because of her wonderful way of dealing with people, she became known as the Angel Nurse.

Rina introduced the two young people and said to herself, "I'm going to work as cupid with those two!"

Maria and Lane danced the evening away until the band stopped playing. Lane suggested that he give Maria a ride home from the wedding party. Even though she was twenty-some years old, Maria felt that she should get the approval of her father in being alone with an unfamiliar man. Juan Cardoza was an old-fashioned man with strong Castillian values which may have been old, but were very meaningful to him and his wife. Juan gladly gave his approval for the couple to leave together.

Lane and Maria slowly drove through town to the area that was known as "Spanish town" where all the African and Mexican American families resided. After sitting and chatting in Lane's car for a while, Maria invited her new friend into the house for a cup of coffee. They had just started sipping their coffee when Maria's parents arrived home. A warm, congenial visit followed as they talked of families and life in general in their local town.

Finally, after a long day for everyone, they all decided to say goodnight. Maria's mother had a good feeling about Lane and suggested he come back soon for a visit with the Cardoza family.

The war years in America, in all communities, created many changes in people's lives. In many families they found much despair and misery. Family life was changed in many ways forever. Because men eighteen and over had to register for the draft, Lane soon received his notice and reported to the Army boot camp for six weeks of basic training.

After boot camp, Lane had a furlough and naturally headed for home to visit his friends, and especially his sweetheart, Maria Cardoza. After a few days, the young couple made a big decision to get married. Lane met with Mr. and Mrs. Cardoza and politely asked for Maria's hand in marriage. The parents readily accepted the proposal.

They knew they had to rush plans for the wedding, as Lane would soon have to return to the army. The Cardozas needed help making arrangements for the wedding and Sam and Rina pitched in to help. A small, but beautiful wedding took place with friends and family attending.

After the wedding, the young couple spent a few days traveling on the train to Lane's next army assignment at Fort Benning, Georgia. The trip to Georgia would be their honeymoon, but they hoped for a better celebration after the war.

Lane reported to jump school at Fort Benning. In addition to jump school, he was assigned to a special communications training group for paratroopers. This was a squad of young men who were all Native Americans. In this group Lane met some other men who also knew the Lakota language.

One of the officers explained to the group that the use of their Indian language would be of value in foreign lands where the enemy had no knowledge of the Lakota language. The United States Intelligence Department thought this would be a huge advantage, especially behind enemy lines in German-occupied countries. After a great deal of training, Lane was assigned to a paratrooper battalion in which he would serve until the end of World War II.

As the war continued, the local economy kept buzzing along. But still people were affected in many ways. Almost every family had a son or daughter in the military. There was always the chance of receiving bad news of the loss of a loved one. For the most part, people kept their spirits up, but they were also eager for a victory and peace at last.

Communications during this time were somewhat limited. A man in the service could mention only brief comments about where he might be. So, a lot of guess work went on as to where a family member was serving his country.

During the midyears of the war, young Lane's next army assignment took him and his battalion to Camp Kilmer, New Jersey. This was extremely tough training and it turned out to be their final preparation to engage the enemy in Europe. At this time Maria thought it best to go home to her family and wait for Lane to return.

A few months later the group was shipped out to England for more special training. Little did they know, their final experience, after all their specialized training, would place them in that famous "Battle of the Bulge."

All military men were warned over and over not to discuss operation details outside their various meetings. Because of these continual warnings and extra security precautions, the soldiers knew that they were going to be a part of something big. And they were—the invasion of Europe.

Twenty

ometimes when Sam needed a little diversion from the
war news and his work at the ranch, he would seek out
several railroad workers who had become good friends.
Once or twice a month they would invite Sam to join them for a
card game or to shoot some pool. Sam enjoyed these times with
his friends, especially their humor and wild stories.

Sam's closest pal was Bill who was better known among his
friends as "Bill the Sharp." Bill earned this nickname because he
was always making some kind of sharp deal for something he
needed. Bill was also a natural storyteller and especially liked to
tell about the escapades of Filthy Fliker.

So, one evening Bill told Sam and his pool hall pals the latest
story about this humorous and fun-loving crew of railroad
workers.

Bill said, "One of the regular runs is to the north toward the
Black Hills. On this run the rail line progresses on a steady
elevation climb. We refer to this run as the 'hill run.' It is a long
and sometimes slow run because of many heavy loads.

"The five of us made a deal in a small town at a stop-over
location. We would rent a shack for our layovers until our next
run home. This shack is very basic, but it costs a lot less than the
local hotel.

"The owner of the shack is Boom Boom Mary. She also owns
two of the local taverns. Boom Boom Mary has a heart of gold and

really likes us. We are a compatible group and we have many fun times together.

"Each of us takes on a chore at the shack to keep it halfway liveable. There's not too much to do, but we all cooperate with the chores. I usually take care of the groceries. I pick up the food at Boom Boom's taverns and she gives us a good price."

Bill then added, "I have to tell you about Filthy Fliker, the chef. Filthy took over the cooking duties as he enjoys being in the kitchen. Sanitation and healthy practices with food aren't always important to this chef. He is just one of those messy guys.

"Filthy's favorite cooking utensil is a huge frying pan. He tosses any type of food into this pan for a meal. After the meal, Filthy cleans the pan by wiping it with a newspaper and then takes it to the stream a few yards behind the shack to scour it with sand from the stream. Then he hangs it on the wall outside by the front door. After it hangs on the wall a few hours, he wipes off the flies and bugs and prepares the next meal.

"While Filthy cooks, he sings his favorite risqué songs. Some of his compositions are quite humorous, but the songs are not the type we take home to the family.

"Once in a while we put our feet down on his bad habits in the kitchen. His worst habit happens when he is in a hurry to cook and he pulls his grimy work boots off and places them with his dirty socks on a shelf right over the wood burning stove. Since he wears a pair of socks several days, a ripe odor lingers over the food on the stove. So we have to remove the boots and socks to the outside when we notice them."

Sam and the other men laughed as they thought about that frying pan and those socks!

Bill chuckled, "You haven't heard the best story yet. One day Filthy dreamed up the idea of building a still in the wooded area behind the shack. We weren't sure what he was making and neither was he. It took him a long time to complete his project.

"He thought since he would end up being a big time booze dealer, he should have a sign at the distillery. After all, he thought he deserved the attention. So, he painted a crude cardboard sign that said F.W. Fliker Distillery, Inc. He nailed it to a pine tree and below it said "No Trespassing."

"Of course this inflated his ego," Bill added, "but there would never be anyone coming by to see his business venture.

"On a day when we were all at the shack, Filthy was working extra hard to finish the still. In the middle of the day he thought he had everything set to start his first batch of whiskey. With all his ingredients in the vat, he was sure that all he needed was additional heat. Fortunately the still was in a clearing away from the shack and not too close to the woods.

"Filthy piled more wood on the blazing fire beneath the bubbling juices of the vat. He was wearing his favorite year-round uniform—long red flannel underwear, long winter socks, and a ten-gallon Stetson—he was sweating like a champ.

"Next to the still were Filthy's magic ingredients, including alcohol and some fermented fruits. They were not a good combination. A few sparks landed on the supplies and some of the paper pieces burst into flames. Filthy jumped and ran in circles trying to control the flames.

"In a couple of minutes the still blew straight up in the air like a shot out of a cannon. Fortunately, it actually blew the fire out. But, a few of the flying sparks landed on Filthy and with the other mixtures that had splashed on him, his red flannels burst into fire spots. Filthy, in his heated misery, ran the twenty yards to the nearby creek and rolled around in the welcomed cool water.

"As he ran by the shack, we could see a streak of fire fly by and of course we ran out to check on him. There he was in the stream, splashing and cussing.

"We asked him what had happened and Filthy calmly said that the damned fruit was too strong and potent for making high quality whiskey that he was accustomed to.

"Late that afternoon the local sheriff came by to see what had happened. Filthy told a wild tale of how he was grilling a wild boar from Australia and the fire and coals just seemed to explode the boar roasting on the stick. The sheriff knew he was dealing with some wild and crazy railroaders, but he believed some of the humorous tales. The case was closed."

Sam and the other men had to wipe tears from their eyes as they were laughing so hard.

Sam saw these railroaders as a truly rare breed of men. They worked hard and lived hard in those days when life was not easy in the western-prairie country. And boy, could they tell stories!

Twenty-one

The war effort put a real strain on all cities and towns during this time of America's growth. Many businesses and companies switched their entire production over to do their part in the war effort. The world had never seen such patriotism develop overnight as it did in America.

With the ration stamp program in full swing for the duration of the war, people found it hard to purchase any number of necessities—gasoline, tires, shoes, toiletries, and worst of all, food items.

Because of the food shortages, victory gardens were started all over the country. Neighbors got together and found open areas and turned them into large vegetable gardens. Cities and towns set up sites all over for its citizens to plant, care for, and harvest the much needed vegetables. Again this was an example of the spirit and know-how of Americans to solve their own problems.

There was a woman who became a good friend of Rina's. She lived on the edge of town with her three children. The woman, Ella Barnes, was a widow, whose husband had been killed in a tragic railroad accident.

Rina met Ella after she had heard about the values of drinking goat's milk. Rina checked this out with Dr. Brown, who recommended the goat's milk as a healthy food. He told Rina about Ella who sold the milk to a few people in the community.

Ella and her children had a small house sitting on about three lots of property. She had a cow, a horse, chickens, and a few goats. So, with what she had, including a great spirit and strong work ethic, she fended for herself quite well.

After the war started, she began to sell more of her vegetables and eggs. She also began telling her customers about the quality of goats' milk. She was good at selling her products and in a short time the milk became quite popular.

Ella had good business sense and slowly, but continually, saved some money. After a couple of years she was able to buy some additional land and her business ventures grew.

With more success, Ella's hard work became known as the business success story of the town and a wonderful example of what people can do for themselves.

One day Ella went downtown to a department store to buy some clothes for her children. From there she went to the bank. Upon entering the bank, a very large paratrooper collided with Ella and her packages flew out of her arms and skidded across the polished floor.

Momentarily stunned and embarrassed, the two stared at each other. The sergeant quickly helped Ella retrieve her packages and apologized for his clumsy movement. After a few words to each other, the two walked together to the banking counter where customers were lined up. Ella and the sergeant got in nearby lines and had a friendly conversation.

Upon completing their business transactions about the same time, the two met again near the front door. The sergeant said, I would like to introduce myself." They stopped in front of the bank and he said, "My name is Herman Goetz and I'm from a large city back East. I feel guilty about our accident and I wondered if you would like to have a cup of coffee with me?"

Ella had been without her husband for a few years and this encounter was quite a change for her. After coffee and some light, friendly conversation, they went on their separate ways. In departing, they agreed it would be nice to see each other again.

Sam's Journey

A few days later, Herman had to make a visit into town. He remembered where Ella said she lived with her three children, so he drove out in the military car he was using that day. As he pulled off the road at Ella's place, he spotted Ella in a nearby field working with a shovel. Herman plodded through the field and yelled a greeting to Ella. She was completely surprised and, being covered with dust and sweat from her hard work, she was a little embarrassed.

They shook hands and Ella invited her new friend to the house for some cold lemonade. Ella was a little flustered at first with her guest, but Herman had a way about himself that quickly relaxed Ella. As the minutes went by, they found that they had many interests in common. Finally, their visit was about over and Herman had to return to his military duties and Ella's children would soon be home from school.

It was easy to see that Ella was happy to have this new friend and she invited him back for a dinner with her family. Herman had to check his work schedule first but they soon set up a dinner date.

Ella prepared an excellent meal for their dinner, and Herman really enjoyed the home cooked meal—his first in several months.

Ella and Herman both enjoyed sports activities and Ella encouraged her children to participate in local team sports whenever possible.

Herman, at the start of the war, was a student athlete at an eastern university. With his size and physical skills he was considered to be a huge success as a college player and pro football prospect. But the draft and World War II completely changed his football future.

Ella's oldest son, Karl, at thirteen and a good-sized boy for his age, was very enthusiastic about playing football and immediately a friendship developed between Karl and Herman.

After an enjoyable evening of conversation the kids went to bed and Herman said good night to his friend Ella.

Over the next few weeks Ella and Herman became very close. In addition, Herman was very good with her children and they developed a fond friendship.

Ella also introduced Herman to Rina and Sam and the two couples got together for card games and socializing.

Six months later Herman just knew he had to have Ella as his bride. Ella accepted Herman's proposal and within the month they were married at the local Lutheran church. It was a beautiful wedding and Rina and other friends organized a celebration party to wish the bride and groom a happy, successful life together

Thirty days later Herman and his airborne unit were sent to Fort Benning, Georgia, for some final training. From the rumbling of rumors among military personnel it was believed their next big jump would be in Italy.

There was much sadness in the small farmhouse on the edge of town and many prayers were said daily for their big, lovable paratrooper whom they missed so much.

Time passed slowly and Ella did not receive any word from her husband. It wasn't until a few months later that a notice came from the army. Ella sat down as she nervously opened the envelope. Tears came to her eyes as she read that Herman's troop might have been captured by a German Panzer unit and put in a prisoner of war camp. The letter said that at this time the whereabouts of the soldiers were unknown.

Ella could not imagine life without Herman. All of her friends and family prayed daily for his safe return.

Twenty-two

Early one morning Sam and Rina were eating breakfast when the phone rang. It was Ella with the exciting news that Herman was on his way home after being released from the prison camp and a hospital stay. Sam, Rina, and Ella immediately started to plan a welcome home celebration for Herman.

When the day arrived, Herman was met at the train depot by his family and many close friends in the community.

Shortly after Herman had time to readjust to civilian life, Sam invited him and his family out to the ranch for dinner. When they finished eating, Sam asked Herman to take a walk with him. As they walked Sam said, "I don't want to pry, but I am interested in anything you can talk about regarding your war experiences."

Herman was reluctant to talk about his capture in Italy, but suddenly he realized that it would be a relief to talk to someone, and Sam was the ideal person with whom to share his story. Sam and Herman sat down on a nearby hillside and Herman told his story about how it all began.

"I woke up that morning, shocked at my surroundings. I was lying on a hard wood bed of sorts with several olive tree branches as a simple mattress. To further my shock, I realized I could not remember how I got to my present situation.

"I moaned slightly and looked to the side of the stone cell I was in. Immediately another soldier jumped to his feet and quickly came to my side.

"Then, six other soldiers were suddenly at my side. They said that they were about to give up on me. I had been out like a light for almost a week. Putting things together, they figured I had a really bad concussion.

"They asked if I remembered anything about our jump since I had been in and out of it and had tried to mumble and talk repeatedly. This was the first time since our jump that I had been awake.

"I told them that I remembered our jump. I remembered losing control and landing in a huge tree upside down. A corporal told me he saw me drop into that tree and that my head banged really hard into a huge branch. They got out of their chutes and found me hanging there upside down and completely knocked out.

"I asked where we were and how we got there. I saw that we were apparently in some type of prison or jail cell.

"They told me how they pulled me from the tree and they knew they had to move fast as they were close to the German infantry.

"In our jump, the eight of us somehow got separated from our group of two hundred troopers. We had flown out of Palermo; in Sicily, and our drop site was just south of Catanzaro, Italy.

"On the morning of the second day after landing, we were surrounded by a squad of German elite Panzer soldiers. We were captured without a shot fired. We were completely surprised.

"At first they told me we would all be shot. But, we lucked out. These Germans reacted to everything like high-level, specially trained professionals—the cream of the German high command that we had been told about.

"We had to march a couple of miles to the small town of Mazzo where we were in a prison for Italian civilian prisoners. That is where I was when I woke up from my delirium.

"We were fed twice a day—mostly olives, bread, squash, and water. We were taken out of our cells once a day for a short time for exercise. We did not see any other soldiers outside our cell, but we thought we heard some voices from time to time that were speaking English.

"We were never threatened or harmed in any way. The days were boring and we couldn't help but wonder what was going to happen to us.

"After being in prison for at least a month, I gathered my comrades close together. I told them that during our break that day I had noticed our three guards whispering to each other. I also noticed the younger of the three was very nervous and the senior man grumbled at the young man in a low voice. As the three talked I thought they did not pay attention to us as usual. I told the men I thought something was about to happen.

"Late that night we heard hollering and screaming outside our jail cell. Then there was the sound of several soldiers running down the hallway outside the cell.

"Quickly the sound of the German soldiers died down and there was no sound at all. The quietness was eerie.

"About five minutes later we heard several huge explosions. Then it stopped. There was not much sleeping for us that night and we were all very tense.

"At sunrise the next day, there was the sound of gunfire close to the prison area. I told the men we should break out of there. If the Germans were still out there, I thought we were in serious trouble. I thought we had lucked out and I gambled that all that noise was from the American infantry.

"We tugged and pulled stones from the cell walls and then tore the wooden cots apart. With those simple tools we attacked the hard, wooden jail door. Finally the door began to splinter. In a fury we ripped the door apart.

"I peeked around the door and looked down the hallway and saw that it was empty. The eight of us slowly went down the hall to a metal door that was partly open. I opened the door and to my surprise I saw fifty or more American soldiers sitting around the small plaza just outside the prison. I quickly told my men of the situation and said that we had better go out slowly and not start a shooting match by surprising them.

"I removed my shirt and slowly opened the door all the way while reaching out and shaking my shirt vigorously. Two soldiers reacted quickly and pointed their carbines at me. I stepped all the way out into the group of soldiers with my hands raised high.

"I was quickly surrounded by ten of the soldiers and led to the middle of the group where a major was going over some maps with other officers.

"I explained to the major that other American soldiers were still inside the open doorway a few feet away. I also said that I thought there were other prisoners inside the prison area.

"The major immediately sent several of his men into the prison to release the Americans. All told, the major and his men released over thirty soldiers from the cells.

"The more seriously hurt soldiers were sent to a medic field site well behind the field of battle. One of my fellow captives told that major that due to my head injury, I should be sent there as well because of my severe pain and headaches.

"Then I was sent back to the rear lines and after a brief examination I was sent to Palermo, Sicily. In Palermo I boarded a hospital ship and returned to the United States."

Herman added, "Thankfully I have recovered from my wounds and am so happy to be home with Ella and our family. I am one of the lucky soldiers to come home."

Sam thanked Herman for sharing his difficult story and for his service to his country and said, "Now it is time for you to get on with your life."

Twenty-three

Sam and his friend and business partner, Cyrus Dutman, usually met three or four times a month to discuss their business concerns and also have some laughs together and trade family stories.

Cyrus was getting on in years and slowing down somewhat. But he still hung on to some old-timer habits. For instance, he always insisted on meeting Sam on horseback near Cyrus's ranch.

On one particular morning, the two friends were sitting by one of Cyrus's chuck wagons watching a few wranglers work with some stallions that Cyrus had just bought at a horse sale.

The two looked up when they heard a car pull up to the site. The area marshal climbed out of his car and was greeted by the two friends. After a few friendly words, the marshal said he was there to deliver some negative news.

The marshal said, "Early this morning I received word from a penitentiary in the East that an inmate, Mac Bruner, was released on parole. Several years earlier Bruner had been considered a no-good and evil man to contend with. Surprisingly, in the last couple of years, he had become a changed man and model prisoner. In his earlier years in prison he had vowed to get revenge on you, Cyrus. The warden remembered that and thought you should be aware of this."

The marshal told Cyrus, "I am sure Mac Bruner probably won't show up, but you and your crew should keep on the lookout for him."

Cyrus and Sam discussed the situation and decided they would have their key cowboys be aware of any questionable people coming around the area.

A week later, Cyrus took off early on horseback to check and repair some fences on his west area pastureland. Cyrus's old Shepherd dog followed along.

Early that evening Anna Dutman was truly alarmed as Cyrus and his favorite hound dog had not returned home for dinner. It was close to sunset when Anna went to tell Sam and Rina of her worry. Sam quickly rounded up some of his key men and they made a quick round of the area on horseback.

Sam also contacted Lone Tall Tree right away to assist in the search for their friend. Lone was an expert at tracking and searching—after all, age-old experts had taught him.

About three miles west of the ranch house, in a long ravine, Shep, Cyrus's old Shepherd hound, was found. The poor dog had been brutally beaten. He had two broken legs and a slit throat. There was no sign of Cyrus or his horse.

Sam and his crew were very upset. It was late by now and very dark so the men could not do much in their search.

Sam got in his old car and drove into town to report the problem to the marshal. Sam's idea was to start searching again early the next morning.

After sharing ideas on where to concentrate their search, it was decided to cover the area south of town. Lone Tall Tree had a gut feeling as to where to go. Lone, in thinking about the kind of man who probably kidnaped Cyrus, felt that he had probably taken Cyrus to Bruner's old familiar grounds down by South Lake.

Lone had his eight men cover the area straight to the south of town. Lone took off ahead of them at a faster pace toward what he thought was the target area.

It was before sunrise and Lone saw a flicker of light about a half mile ahead of him in a gully. Lone got off his horse, took his hunting rifle, rechecked his pistol, and headed for the light about three hundred yards ahead of him.

Lone stayed low to the top of the knoll overlooking a campfire at the bottom of the gully. There were five men stretched out on bedrolls spread around a campfire. A few feet from the smoldering fire was an old farm wagon. Lone moved closer to the wagon and he spotted his old friend, Cyrus, tied to one of the rear wheels of the wagon. Cyrus was in a sitting position and his arms were tied to the upper part of the wheel, and his head was hanging down on his chest.

At this point, Lone knew that he had to be very careful of his next move. He decided to get Cyrus out of there somehow but he debated waiting for his friends about a mile behind him. Lone decided he had no time to waste. He took a small stone and threw it at the campfire. It made a slight noise but there wasn't a move or sound among the sleepers.

The warrior spirit in Lone took over his thinking and decision-making. He quietly went behind the wagon and crawled under it behind the wheel where Cyrus was. He pulled out his hunting knife and laid it on the ground. He then gently covered Cyrus's mouth and whispered in his ear. At first he wasn't sure Cyrus could understand what was going on. Cyrus finally recognized the familiar voice behind him.

Lone cut the ropes from the wagon and then cut the rope around Cyrus's ankles. He then dragged his friend around the wagon and slowly they walked away from the campsite.

Soon the rest of the search party approached the site. They gathered the whole group and sat down around Cyrus, deciding how they would surround the bad guys and overtake them.

Cyrus sat up from his resting position, and said he was going to take part in the action against these varmints. The marshal said no to that idea, but Sam spoke up and said, "Let him join us. I'll be his partner in this fight and I promise you nothing will go wrong. After what he's been through I think he deserves the chance to face these guys eye-to-eye."

The marshal spread his group of twenty-five men around the sleeping bad guys. Cyrus said he wanted to be the one to give the wake up call to the sleepers. He would stand by Bruner and blast off a shotgun close to his ear. They figured that should get his attention!

The marshal placed at least three men standing over each bad dude. Cyrus and Sam found Bruner. Cyrus, the rugged old cowboy, leaned over his enemy, pointed the shotgun up to the sky and blasted away.

And what a shocking blast it was to the sleepers! Bruner rolled over and started to jump to his feet. Cyrus was ready for him. He swung the rifle butt into the man's face with full force breaking his nose. Bruner dropped to the ground like a sack of potatoes falling off a wagon.

Once they had the bad guys securely tied up and placed on their backs near the campfire, the marshal made it very clear as to what the law's charge was against them. All of them were charged with kidnaping and the threat of murder.

Bruner was his old self and spouted off many obscenities and threats. He was also certainly shocked that the search party had caught up with him as quickly as they had.

The marshal made Cyrus and Sam sit down on the edge of the group to hear the facts about the threats and abuses against Cyrus. First of all," Cyrus said, "Bruner is absolutely insane. I couldn't talk to him at all. He was even brutal to his own men. If they asked any questions, he would knock them off their feet. The guy has no mercy for anyone. His plan was to get money from my family and me; he really thought he could pull it off. He even showed me a disguise, which included a red wig, a beard, and a walking stick. Inside the stick was a long, razor-sharp blade. This crazy man said that tomorrow morning he planned to walk right into the bank, go to the bank president's office, and take out two hundred thousand dollars. That money was to pay for my life."

Cyrus continued, "That was basically the whole plan which was dumb, and clearly the thinking of an insane man. Thank God you men showed up just in time. This man was ready to shoot his way out of town and a lot of people could have been hurt."

With that information the marshal said that the next day they would find the answers to a few more questions he had. Bruner and his gang would then be headed back to prison and the marshal was sure Bruner would spend the rest of his life behind bars.

Cyrus was taken to the hospital for a complete examination and bed rest was ordered for three days before he could be released.

Dr. Brown said he was very impressed with Cyrus's condition after the mean treatment he had received. The doctor said the old cowboy's lifestyle over the years kept him in good physical condition and probably saved his life. The doctor also ordered Cyrus to stay off his horse for a couple of weeks. Anna knew that would be a tough job. Rina suggested hiding his boots and hat thinking that might force him to rest a while.

Cyrus did recover and Anna did not know whether to laugh or cry as she watched her favorite cowboy saddle up and take off for a ride across the prairie he loved so much.

A few days later, Sam and Rina helped Anna organize a party to celebrate Cyrus's recovery from his recent ordeal. The party was at Anna and Cyrus's ranch on a late summer night.

It was a wonderful party with an abundance of food, drink, music, dancing, and fun to celebrate with their old friend Cyrus Dutman.

Later that night, after many of the guests had left, a few close friends sat around the campfire with Cyrus and Anna. The talk was warm and friendly and many humorous stories were told.

In a lull in the conversation Anna said, "Cyrus, as we have been sitting here in our wonderful little part of the world, I'm reminded of how far we have come from our humble beginning.

Look at where we are now. Right at this minute with our home and our friends, we have much to be thankful for."

All was quiet and Cyrus spoke up in a calm steady voice, "Yes, it has been a long, hard struggle to get where we are.

"But, I'm not the only one that has accomplished good things in our great country. I know that my friend Sam also had to struggle to make his way here."

Sam spoke up and said, "Let's not talk about me, this is Cyrus's party. Yes, it has been a struggle to improve our lives, but to make our country great we have all worked hard for the many good things we enjoy today."

It was late in the evening when the party broke up and everyone left in a happy mood after celebrating with their friends, Cyrus and Anna.

Twenty-four

The fall season of that year was an especially nice time with very enjoyable weather. But everyone knew what was coming. The prediction was for a very cold, rugged winter.

By November, Old Man Winter had come to the plains area in full force—with wind, rain, snow and ice. In January the temperature was often well below zero degrees.

On a severely cold morning that month, Cyrus got up earlier than usual. Anna fixed Cyrus his usual big breakfast and he then put on his longjohns and extra socks.

Anna asked him, "What are you doing?"

Cyrus answered, "I just have to ride out and make sure our cowboys are okay. It is cold out there."

Cyrus got on his favorite horse, Picture. Cyrus named the horse Picture because of its great beauty. They headed west at a slow walk for about two miles from the ranch house. The ever-surefooted cow pony stepped on a sliver of frozen snow and stumbled to the hard, frozen tundra in a quick jolt for the two of them. As they fell, Cyrus landed on his side and Picture rolled over on Cyrus's legs. The weight of the falling horse sprained both of Cyrus's ankles.

The horse slipped, but managed to get to its feet. Cyrus was in much pain. After resting a few minutes, he crawled to the horse and somehow pulled himself to his feet, but he could not pull himself up and onto the saddle. Because of the cold, miserable weather and his injured ankles, Cyrus knew he faced a serious problem. He was all alone and out in the wide-open countryside. He knew he had to somehow get back to the ranch home.

Cyrus remembered stories of the past when cowboys had accidents on the range in similar situations and sometimes froze to death.

Somehow, Cyrus pulled himself up to the side of the horse. Once on his feet and holding on to the saddle, Picture slowly walked in the direction of the ranch house. In great pain Cyrus struggled to within one hundred yards of the ranch house. He hollered a few times hoping to get some attention, but the howling wind cut off his voice. Finally, after struggling for about another hour, one of his ranch hands came along and helped Cyrus to the house. Anna was very worried about her husband and scolded him by saying, "Shame on you, you old, wild man. You are not a young bronco-buster anymore!"

Anna got Cyrus in bed and fed him her famous chicken soup. She then called Dr. Brown. After explaining the situation and Cyrus's condition, the doctor said he would be at the ranch within the hour.

Meanwhile, Cyrus had developed a bad chest cold and he told Anna that he was so cold and could not get warm. Dr. Brown finally arrived at the ranch house after a fierce battle with the weather conditions in his old Ford sedan.

After examining Cyrus, the doctor decided to get Cyrus to the hospital right away. They bundled up Cyrus and with the help of a couple of cowboys, they carried him out to the car.

It was a tough ride back to town where Cyrus was admitted to the hospital and immediately placed on oxygen. After a week in the hospital Cyrus showed slight improvement. Then his severe chest cold turned worse and he developed pneumonia in both lungs.

After another week of close supervision, the doctor told Anna, "What a fighter this old cowboy is!"

Several days later Cyrus again showed a slight improvement. Feeling a little better one day, he decided he was tired and bored with the hospital. He demanded that one of the young nurses should get his boots and clothes—he was going home!

Once he got on his feet he discovered he had trouble standing because his nearly broken ankles were not healed. Dr. Brown and Anna quickly calmed down Cyrus. The doctor made a deal with Cyrus and told him he would get him home by the weekend if he would behave himself and not scare the young nurses with wild man threats!

That weekend they bundled up Cyrus again for the ride out to his ranch. Fortunately it was a fairly warm day. It was showing signs of a possible early spring that year.

Cyrus was more content being at home and being able to talk with his many ranch hands. But Cyrus was still having some problems breathing and Dr. Brown was becoming more concerned with Cyrus's overall condition.

Cyrus started to slowly walk around the house using two canes for support. As he was hobbling around the house one day, he decided it looked very nice outside and he went out on the front porch for some fresh air. It was now the middle of February and still capable of a quick weather change. Cyrus sat on the porch a few minutes and Anna came out and scolded him for being so foolish for sitting outside in this still very cold weather.

Back inside, Anna put her old wrangler back to bed. She noticed at once that his body seemed quite cold and the cold air outside seemed to affect his lungs and breathing.

Cyrus then seemed to get weaker and weaker and was admitted back in the hospital. After a couple of weeks in the hospital, Cyrus Dutman's strength gave up the battle and late one night he went to sleep, never to wake again.

Sam and Rina sat down with Anna to help plan the funeral for Cyrus. Anna decided to put Cyrus to rest on a small hill a couple hundred yards west of the ranch house. She said that was a favorite spot to Cyrus, a place where he had watched the beautiful sunsets of his beloved western plains.

After a short service at a local church, Anna had Cyrus take his last ride in an old ranch wagon pulled by two of Sam's beautiful Belgian work horses to the burial site on that small hill west of the ranch house. A few words were spoken at the grave site and neighbors and friends slowly left the final resting place of Cyrus. Anna was surprised at the large number of people attending the service; more than a hundred people came by to say goodbye to an old friend. Anna's close friends knew she was going to be a lonely woman without Cyrus around the ranch. So Willow Tall Tree had two of her daughters stay for several days with Anna

As they were driving home, Sam said, "Rina, Cyrus was not only a great friend, he was also a wonderful mentor. I learned so much from him. I'll miss him."

Twenty-five

After a short time of mourning, Anna reminded Sam that it was Cyrus's desire to have Sam take over the total management of the ranch. Anna had complete faith in Sam and knew he would do an excellent job on her behalf.

Sam realized he had taken on a large responsibility. With his various other business interests, he faced a real challenge, but he knew he could handle it. However, he also knew he would need extra help.

By now Jake was a well-rounded ranch hand. Due to Sam's supervision, he became an excellent handler and trainer of horses. Sam gave his son a few easy jobs and continually added new responsibilities. Rina worried that Sam was too tough on their son, but Sam's answer was that he was making him into a man.

Over the past few years, Jake thoroughly accepted his job as a ranch hand, but after graduation from high school his mother encouraged him to go to college. Jake thought it over and decided to give college a try. He enrolled at a university in the eastern part of the state. Although not a top student, Jake did well academically.

After one year at the university Jake met with his parents and said, "I am not going to continue with college. I miss life on the ranch where I grew up and the wide-open spaces of the western plains."

Sam and Rina were disappointed, but Jake added, "As young as I am, I may want to try college again later, but I feel I'm not ready at this time for an academic life."

So, Jake returned to working on the ranch, and under Sam's guidance, became very adept at working with all types of horses. Various cow hands on the ranch often said that he was just like his old man. One thing Jake really enjoyed was teaching people to ride a horse or to improve their riding skills.

One beautiful fall day Rina invited Anna, Willow Tall Tree, Maria Walker, and Ida Lemter to her home for coffee and cake.

Ida was fairly new to the area. She was from the East and was a high school history teacher. In the last year she had become friends with the older women.

As they talked, the conversation turned to their men friends and husbands who were doing work that involved horses. Ida realized that she was the only one there who did not know anything about horses and how to ride them.

The other women were surprised at this and told Ida some very humorous stories about their experiences with horses. Ida then said she not only did not know about horses, but that she was very frightened of them as they were such huge animals.

Willow spoke up and said, "We've got to change that. If you live around here you should learn to ride. I know how we can help you. Rina has her son Jake who is one of the best at teaching people how to ride a horse. Let's give it a try."

Ida said she would think it over. But over the next several days, Ida's friends would keep suggesting riding lessons for her. Finally, Ida gave in and decided to meet the wrangler who could teach her how to ride, but she knew this would be quite a challenge.

Meanwhile, Rina told Jake that she had a new student for him. Jake did not pay much attention and thought he would be dealing with one of the local school marms. He was not excited about teaching some old maid teacher!

Rina purposely left out a few things about Ida. She did not want to oversell the new student who was actually a very pretty young woman with dark brown hair and big hazel eyes. She was also very intelligent.

On the day of Ida's first riding lesson, Maria picked up Ida after school and they drove to Rina's ranch. As they approached the ranch house, they saw Rina puttering around her flower bed by the front porch. The three women sat down on the front porch and visited for a few minutes. Rina then excused herself and went to the barnyard to find Jake. Rina found him behind the barn and told him to get to the house and meet Ida. Mother and son walked to the front porch and Rina introduced the two young people.

Jake was surprised at the young lady before him. He said to himself, *"What an old maid teacher, wow!"*

Jake led Ida to the main barnyard where he had a beautiful black mare saddled up and ready for a walk. Jake told Ida that this was Sal, a very gentle eight-year-old horse. Jake gave the reins to Ida and they walked the horse out past the barn for a few hundred yards. They talked in easy voices and Jake spoke about how to get along with a horse.

Ida became more and more relaxed standing by the horse as she listened to Jake. Jake then helped Ida climb up on the horse. He told Ida he would walk along beside her as he instructed her how to use the reins.

They turned around and walked back toward the barn. As they slowly walked, Jake told stories about his experiences with horses. By the time they got to the barn and Jake helped Ida off the horse, she was very relaxed. They sat on a log by the barnyard and talked of Ida's experience with the ride. She said she really enjoyed it and was surprised at how well things went.

Jake said, "This is a good beginning and if you are happy with your experience we should schedule some more lessons." Ida agreed and they set up a regular time for more rides.

Jake walked Ida back to the ranch house and they visited with Rina and Marie. Jake excused himself and went back to work.

On the ride back to town Maria asked Ida how she felt about her riding lesson. Ida answered, "That cowboy is a very good teacher and I'm anxious for the next session."

Over the next few weeks the cowboy and the young teacher became friendlier as they found they had many similar interests.

One day as Rina and Maria were visiting, Maria said, "Maybe I should not say this, but lately every time Ida and I drive back to town after she and Jake have been riding, I notice a real glow in Ida's face and the way she speaks. I think we are witnessing the beginning of a love affair."

Rina replied, "I have noticed the same thing with Jake, but I did not want to become a nosy mother."

Ida and Jake were indeed becoming more than just good friends. Soon the horseback lessons came to an end, but the two saw each other on a regular basis. In addition, they enjoyed taking horseback rides together to explore the great prairie country.

A teacher friend of Ida's was getting married that weekend and a party was organized for the newlyweds. Ida naturally invited Jake to be her escort to the party. After a beautiful wedding ceremony, all the guests departed to the town's main social hall.

During the merriment and celebrating, the new bride, in a teasing way, cornered Ida and Jake, and in front of several of their friends asked Jake, "When are you going to make this beautiful woman your bride?"

Ida and Jake both blushed and moved quickly away to the dance floor.

After the party was over and when Jake was driving Ida home she said, "I'm sorry about my friend teasing us tonight. I think she had too much champagne to drink."

Jake quickly parked the car on the side of the street. He put his arm around Ida and pulled her closer to him. He said, "That friend of yours sure made me do some thinking about us."

Ida half-jokingly said, "Well, isn't that nice!"

Jake then blurted out, "We have been together a lot these past months and Ida, I have grown to love you deeply. I don't want to be away from you. I want you to be my wife. Please, please, say you will marry me."

Ida was quiet for a moment and then, with tears in her eyes, she said, "Jake, my love, I want to be your wife and I want you to be my husband. Yes, yes, let's get married!"

It was late at night with a full moon and Jake said, "I'm taking you home to tell my folks about our plans."

The two young lovers pulled up to the ranch house and noticed a light on in the kitchen. Sam and Rina were sitting at the table when Jake and Ida came in. After their greetings were over Jake told his parents about the big decision he and Ida had made. Sam and Rina both jumped out of their chairs to embrace the two young lovers.

After many hugs and kisses they all sat down and Sam brought out a jug of wine and made a toast of congratulations to the happy couple.

After more conversation Rina told Ida to tell her how she could help with the wedding plans. Ida said, "As you know, my parents live in Kansas City and I want them to be involved with the plans. I am so excited! I feel like I am floating on a cloud. I just don't know what or how to think of anything."

Rina came to Ida's rescue and suggested that since it was quite late and it had been a busy day, they should call it a night and get together in a day or two to do their planning.

They all bid their good nights and Jake drove Ida back to her apartment and wished his future bride a good night of rest and dreams about their future together.

Twenty-six

A few days later, Rina and Ida got together with a few friends to discuss the future wedding. Ida said she did not want a big wedding or party. After this meeting, Ida realized she had to contact her parents about her upcoming wedding to Jake.

Ida's parents were born and raised in Poland and still believed in some old-world customs. So, Ida was concerned about how they would react to the wedding plans.

Ida wrote a long letter to her parents and she immediately received a long letter in response. Her parents were happy for her and Ida was somewhat surprised at how supportive they were. The parents requested that Ida come home to talk about the big event. They, of course, wanted her to have the wedding in Kansas City. After discussing things with Jake, he said, "I'll go with you to Kansas City."

So, off they went to visit Ida's parents. The get-together went well. Ida's family immediately fell in love with Jake. Jake and Ida's father related to each other very well. After getting to know each other better the older man asked, "Jake, are you sure you're not Polish?"

Ida finally agreed with her mother's request to have the wedding in Kansas City the following May. So, plans were made and everyone was happy for the future marriage of the young couple.

All the friends from the West understood Ida's parents wanting the wedding in Kansas City. It would be some distance away, but many people planned to attend.

Sam, with his business connections with the railroad, set up a deal on transportation for their local friends to get a discount on their train fare to Kansas City.

Sam thought of several old friends and business acquaintances that he should send early wedding invitations to, especially his friend Vito Rozzi in Chicago. Sam sent these invitations early as these were very busy people who would appreciate an early notice of the wedding.

The first response to the wedding invitation was from Vito Rozzi. He told Sam and Rina how pleased he was for the invitation. He also told Sam he had a couple of things he needed advice on which they could discuss at the wedding.

For Ida and Jake, the time seemed to go very slowly as they were anxious for the big day. The days and weeks went by and finally the wedding day was there.

There was a huge crowd at the wedding to see the beautiful bride and handsome groom take their wedding vows. After the wedding there was a fine celebration party at a hotel ballroom in the downtown area. The guests ate dinner, drank much champagne, and danced until late in the evening.

It was close to midnight when Vito Rozzi approached Sam. Vito waited until this late hour to talk to Sam because he did not want to interfere with Sam as he visited his many guests.

Vito said, "I do not want to take you from your other guests, but I would like to discuss a matter with you. Maybe we should get together in the morning."

Sam sensed his friend was anxious to talk so he said, "Let's talk tonight and then if we need to, we can finish our discussion in the morning at breakfast."

Vito agreed to this and the two went to a vacant table in the corner of the ballroom. The two friends sat down and Vito quickly told Sam, "I'm sure you remember my sister's son, Tony.

He's a young man who has continually been in and out of trouble. He served in the army and became a more disciplined person, but he is still floundering in life. He has a quick temper and continually gets into trouble.

"Right now he is mixed up with a young woman who is giving him trouble. She claims she is pregnant and that Tony is the father. We have checked into her background and have found that she has pulled this type of thing before and it is a scam. She is a real loser and I don't want Tony getting into this mess any further."

Vito added, "Right now my sister and I have decided to help Tony leave Chicago and move out west. The young man needs a drastic change of scenery in his life. As I see it, it can be a real opportunity for him compared to what he might be facing in Chicago. Sam, will you help us get Tony situated out in your area somewhere?"

Sam wanted to help his friend, but told Vito "I would like to think things over until the morning. I am tired after the big wedding day, but I am sure we can work out a plan for Tony." Sam also wanted to get Rina's thoughts on this situation.

So, early the next morning, the friends got together to discuss Tony's future. Sam raised the question of how Tony would feel about such a drastic move from a big city life to a slower lifestyle in the wide-open prairie country in the West.

Vito answered, "After some serious discussions, Tony agreed his future was very bleak if he did not make the move. Also, my sister is worried sick about her son and doesn't know how to help him."

After some more talk, Sam said that he and Rina would help Tony get started out west. Sam said that Vito should talk to Tony and explain to him that he must start out with the basic jobs on the ranch and that his work would be hard and tough. He also emphasized that Tony must be a team worker and cooperate at all times.

They all agreed to sit down with Tony and work out a schedule for his trip to Sam and Rina's ranch.

With the wedding celebration over and the new bride and groom on their honeymoon, all the guests left to go their separate ways and return to their homes.

Twenty-seven

Two weeks later, Sam and Rina met Tony at the local train station. They picked up Tony's two suitcases and drove out to the ranch. Tony found the prairie country very interesting and asked lots of questions about the area.

They got to the ranch and had Tony stay in the ranch house that first night. The next day Tony would be moved into the cowboy's bunkhouse. The rest of the afternoon Sam gave Tony a brief tour of the ranch and concluded it by introducing Tony to Willy Gorman, the ranch foreman.

Sam told Tony that the next day he would be working with Willy. He also informed Tony to pay close attention to Willy and how he did things as a cowpoke. He added, "Willy is the hardest, toughest cowboy that I know. If you learn anything from Willy, you'll be learning the right way."

The next day started right after sunrise and they worked almost until sunset. Tony worked very hard and Sam was impressed with the way he worked.

Sam told Tony, "Next week you will be working with horses to learn the basic skills in handling them."

After a few days, Sam and Willy sat down with Tony and had a heart-to-heart talk about Tony and his work. Sam was very pleased with the way the young man from the city was adjusting to his work. Sam noticed the young fellow was not a big talker, but was always friendly and polite. Sam also liked the fact that

Tony asked many questions. Overall, Sam and Willy were very pleased with their new cowboy and glad that he got along well with the other cowpokes.

When Ida and Jake returned home from their honeymoon, they made their residence in Sam and Rina's town house, and Jake drove his old Ford to work at the ranch every day.

Sam encouraged Jake to do what he could to help Tony out as a new ranch hand. Fortunately, Jake and Tony got along well with each other and before long they became very good friends.

Later, on a beautiful warm day, Rina was in front of her ranch house puttering around her flower garden. She happened to look up from the garden and to see Tony sitting on a log by the corral. Rina said to herself, *Tony's off from work now and I wonder what he is doing.* She looked a little closer and saw that he had something across his knees and it looked like he had a pencil or pen in his hand.

Rina slowly walked to the corral and as she got close to Tony she saw that he had a large piece of cardboard on his knees with paper on it. He also had a pencil in his hand and Rina noticed several pencil stubs on the ground.

By now, Tony noticed Rina's presence and immediately stood up to greet her. As Tony stood, he dropped his pencil and laid the cardboard on the log.

Rina asked Tony what he was doing and Tony replied, "It was a beautiful day and I decided to sit in the warm sunshine and doodle on some scratch paper."

Rina asked if she could see what he was doodling as she was very curious. She said, "I find myself doing the same thing at times when I am bored."

Tony said he did not have much to show, but he would share what he had been doing. He picked up the cardboard and she saw the piece of paper taped to it. On the paper Tony had sketched various parts of a couple of horses in the barn area. There was a side view of a black stallion, the head of a Pinto pony, and different sketches of horses' eyes. He also had done a sketch of a barn owl.

Rina was absolutely amazed at what she was viewing. In fact, she was almost breathless. Rina knew a little about art and painters because she often visited the art museum and art galleries when she had lived in Philadelphia.

Rina asked Tony, "What is this paper you used?"

Tony replied "Whenever I saw wasted paper I would save it to sketch on."

Rina asked, "You mean to say you have other sketches like this?"

Tony said, "I have a few but I have thrown away most of them."

Rina could hardly believe the talent that was before her. She had many questions running through her mind about this young man. She wondered about how long he had been "doodling" like this.

Tony told her, "I have been doing this since I was in grade school, but I used to get in trouble with this. I would get bored in class and would not do my lessons and would just spend my time drawing things. I attended a strict Catholic school in Chicago that was very disciplined with its students. Therefore, I was always berated for wasting my time with my drawings. Because of this, I kept my enjoyment of drawing to myself."

Rina then asked, "You have not had any art lessons, have you?"

Tony replied, "No, I have not. But I have visited museums and art galleries to get a better feel for art."

Rina told Tony that she was thankful that he shared his drawings with her. She then added, "I think you should keep up with your sketching. You have a wonderful talent—don't waste it."

Rina was very impressed with Tony and felt strongly that she should help develop his talent. That night after dinner, Rina told

Sam of her interest in helping Tony develop his talent in drawing and painting, but that she wasn't sure what she could do.

Sam was quite surprised that a rough neck man like Tony could have such an artistic talent. After listening to Rina and thinking of her sincere interest in helping the young man, Sam said, "Let's tell this story to Ida. She might know of an art teacher at the high school who could advise Tony and point him in the right direction."

Rina thought Sam had a good idea. She decided to visit with Ida the next day after Ida's last class at the high school. Ida said she was good friends with the art teacher and that they should go see her right away.

That night Rina and Sam invited Tony over to their house to discuss the art teacher and their plan. Rina spoke to Tony and he agreed to meet with the art teacher. So, the next day Lisa met with Tony and they talked for two hours about many things. Lisa had a talent of communicating with young people and she learned many surprising things about this young man.

Lisa looked at all of Tony's sketches and, like Rina, was quite surprised at his ability. She knew that there was a real raw talent there.

Lisa and Tony then went to talk to Rina and Sam. They gathered around Rina's dining room table and Lisa spoke of what she could do to help Tony.

Lisa said, "I do some painting in my spare time. I then take some of my favorite paintings to a friend in Denver who has an art gallery. My friend, Ralif Spanola, sells my paintings for me. Sometimes Ralif takes an interest in a young person with talent and helps develop their natural talent to a higher level."

Lisa then added, "Tony would have to visit and spend some time with the dealer in Denver. It is up to Tony if he wants to be involved in this venture. It will take some time and dedication on his part but I strongly believe he has a talent, maybe a great talent. So, if Tony agrees, I will get in touch with my friend in Denver."

124

After Tony showed his desire to explore this opportunity, Lisa communicated with Ralif Spanola in Denver and the art dealer agreed to devote some time to appraise Tony and his potential.

So, Tony headed for Denver for a new adventure. All of his friends at the ranch wished him well and he promised to keep in touch with these fine people who had been so good to him.

Lisa made the train trip to Denver with Tony. As they traveled over the prairie land, Lisa gave Tony many tips on what to expect at the art gallery.

When they arrived in Denver, they went directly to the art gallery. Tony was quite surprised when they rode up to the beautiful building where the gallery was located.

Lisa introduced the two men and they sat down in a reception area to talk. Then Ralif took Tony and Lisa on a tour of the gallery. Tony was surprised at what he was seeing—a two-story building with spectacular paintings, sketches, and drawings of everything imaginable. Tony wondered how there could be so much beauty and talent in one place.

They finished the tour and went to Ralif's office. Ralif laid out the schedule that Tony would follow for the next week and then they would sit down and decide if they should continue.

Ralif could tell that Tony was impressed with what he saw in the gallery. He explained to Tony that some of the art objects placed around the gallery were to entice certain types of customers to buy. Ralif said, "In my sense of business, I don't want people to leave without buying. The art items you are viewing here are very different and special items from other lands. They seem to appeal to a different type of art lover. I have them on display to keep people looking. Our main business is the pictures, sketches, and paintings. The more I have, the more I sell."

At this point Lisa commented, "Ralif must follow the philosophy of a famous painter who once said, 'Give me a gallery and I'll fill the art centers and the art lovers will benefit from our many gifts'."

They finished the day with Ralif taking them to one of Denver's finest restaurants. Lisa pointed out to Tony several outstanding paintings on the wall of the main dining room. Lisa told Tony that Ralif had sold these paintings to the restaurant.

Ralif, in his modest way, admitted to this and added, "This is another part of my gallery business. I also have some contacts throughout the business community that I've sold paintings to."

After working with Tony for two weeks, Tony proved to be a real diamond in the rough. Ralif felt that he had found an extraordinary talent and made a special position for Tony in his gallery operation.

Tony seemed to have found his place in life. From being a rowdy rough neck to living in Denver and studying in an art gallery, he found it hard to believe. He asked himself, *How can I ever show my appreciation to Rina and Sam for steering me in the right direction?*

So, Tony was on his way to a new lifestyle. After a year of working under Ralif's supervision, Tony was quite successful. Word got around the area about the young man's ability. The very wealthy people of the area discovered Tony's talent and made very handsome payments for his paintings, especially his portraits.

Everything was going just as Ralif had planned. Soon after that first year, Ralif put on an art show. People were invited from all over. There were a few other very talented artists in the show, but Tony was the main feature.

The art show was well received. Ralif had done a fantastic job of putting the show together. The art lovers attending the event came through by spending big dollars for the artwork on display.

Before the show, Tony asked Ralif, "What do I do at the show?"

Ralif replied, "Just stand around and meet and greet people. Help them to more champagne and be nice to them. If you do that, your paintings will sell and so will our other artwork."

Tony Castini was a handsome man in his tuxedo and in a very humble way was a huge success. Tony, on that night, had arrived in the art world.

Twenty-eight

few weeks after the art show, Tony borrowed Ralif's car
and drove to Sam and Rina's ranch for an overdue visit.
Sam and Rina planned a party with a few of Tony's
friends to welcome him back on his brief visit.

The party was a happy occasion with lots of food and drink
and much joy in visiting with their friend Tony, the artist.

Rina and Sam apologized for not attending the art show.
They were so happy to know of Tony's success. Ralif had sent a
letter to them telling of their successful show and how delighted
he was at having Tony be a part of his art business.

During the party, Tony excused himself for a short time and
went out to the car in front of the house. He returned to the
living room where everyone had gathered. He had a large, flat
package in his hands which was wrapped in a thin cloth material.
He had Sam and Rina sit down and he told them he brought this
gift to them in hopes that they would enjoy it.

Together Rina and Sam removed the cloth wrapping and
before them was a beautiful painting. Tony told them this was
something he did in his spare time at the art gallery. The painting
showed Rina and Sam's ranch house with their white picket
fence surrounding the front yard. The scene showed a gorgeous
sunset behind the house with all sorts of bright and brilliant
colors. It depicted the type of sunset that Rina and Sam enjoyed
so many times as they strolled out on the prairie to view their

favorite sites they loved so much. The painting was breathtaking and it was easy to see that each stroke of the artist's brush was done with love.

After everyone in the room had seen the painting, there was a silence and not a word was spoken. Then Rina stood and went to Tony with tears in her eyes. Sam also went to Tony to show his appreciation.

Tony, in a humbling voice, said, "This is my token of appreciation for all you have done for me. You have helped me find a true happiness in life. Thank you."

The party ended late in the evening and everyone left with a happy feeling toward each other and wished Tony much success in his future.

Tony stayed a couple more days at the ranch. He spent some time making sketches of a variety of local people—cowboys, members of the Tall Tree family, and local townspeople. He planned to use the sketches to paint a series of western plains people who typify those who settled and developed the great prairie country.

Tony then said goodbye to his dear friends and headed back to his world of art and the new challenges ahead of him.

Twenty-nine

On a beautiful late spring day, Sam and Rina drove into town. Rina had a school board meeting to attend, and Sam had some ranch business to take care of.

Sam found a parking space near the city hall. As Sam climbed out of his car, he noticed the city mayor approaching him. Sam always liked the mayor, Clem Zachma, and thought he was a good leader for the town. He was the younger brother of Gil Zachman, a former outstanding lawman for the region. Sam admired Clem and thought he was a good mayor for the town.

After exchanging pleasantries, the mayor told Sam, "I was looking for you; I'd like to invite you to my office. I know this is short notice, but there are two men from the East who want to talk to you. Please join us. We won't take up too much of your time."

Sam was surprised and asked Clem what this was about. Clem replied, "Sam, I think you should ask them."

Sam said, "I will, as long as I'm not in trouble." This brought out a couple of laughs.

The mayor introduced the visitors, Ray Kamin and Paul Grillo. The two men explained that they were there representing the state's conservative political party.

Sam asked, "What do you want of me?"

The two men spoke in very eloquent voices and Sam was sure they were both lawyers as they were very smooth in their presentation.

Kamin, the senior of the two men, told Sam, "Our political party is very impressed with your business experiences and overall popularity in this part of the state. We are also aware of your conservative lifestyle and beliefs."

Grillo spoke up and said, "I do not think you know just how well respected you are by so many people."

Sam replied, "I don't think you are here for a popularity contest. Are you here for a donation or what?"

Kamin, after a chuckle said, "You are right, Sam. I'll put everything right on the table. We will go into more detail later, but we are here to see how you feel about out state's political situation and specifically we want to know if you would you be interested in running for political office."

At this point, Sam stood up and said, "Are you crazy? I really don't know much about politics."

The mayor told Sam to sit down and relax and not to get so excited.

Sam asked the two guests, "What political office are you talking about?"

Kamin said, "Sam, we are talking out of deep respect. There are several people in our party who want you to consider running for State Senator representing the western part of the state."

The next several minutes were spent on the discussion of campaigning, timing of the elections, money raising, and answering Sam's questions.

At this point Sam replied, "This discussion has been fascinating to say the least. Right now I am not sure what to think about all of this. I certainly appreciate that you are thinking of me, but I'll have to discuss this with my wife who is my number one partner in life."

Kamin answered, "We want you to do just that. We also know of your wife's abilities and know she would be an asset in a political campaign."

Grillo pointed out to Sam, "Please keep this meeting confidential. We'd like to hear from you within thirty days, if possible. Sam, we want you to know there are some very powerful people in our organization who think that if you run for state senator it could be a step to higher political responsibilities."

Sam gave Grillo a very hard look and said, "What does that mean?"

Kamin told Sam, "This is a little premature, but the powerful people we spoke of think this is a stepping stone to the governor's office for Samuel Rignez."

Sam ran these comments through his mind and said, "I appreciate all the things you have told me, but right now it is almost too much to really think about or totally understand."

The two men from the eastern area of the state said, "Let's meet within the month and discuss this further. We know we have thrown a lot at you in a short time, so please consider our proposal. We want you on our team to serve our people of this area as we know you can."

As the meeting adjourned Grillo said, "Sam, we have a mutual friend—Vito Rozzi. Vito and I grew up together in the same neighborhood in Chicago. He sends you his greetings."

Sam met Rina as she was leaving her school board meeting. As they walked to their car, Rina told Sam about her meeting but she noticed that he was not paying much attention to her. This wasn't like Sam, as he always showed sincere interest in such matters.

Rina stopped Sam and grabbed his arm and said, "Something is bothering you. Is something wrong? You have not heard a word I've said."

Sam apologized to Rina and said, "Let's get in the car and I will bring you up to date. Everything is all right, but there is a lot to discuss."

As they drove to the ranch, Sam spelled out his story of the surprise visitors from the East.

Rina hung on to every word as Sam brought out all the details that he could remember from his talk with the two political visitors. All of a sudden, Sam stopped the car and said he was worn out from the experience.

Rina was speechless for a few minutes and then asked question after question about the proposal that was presented to Sam. Finally, after they relaxed for a few minutes, they continued on their way to the ranch.

As they approached the ranch house Sam said, "This will be a long night. We have a lot to discuss, and we will have to bring Jake in on this. If we accept their proposal, it will really change our lives."

That evening Sam and Rina invited Jake and Ida out to the ranch for a visit. As they sat around the kitchen table, Jake sensed that Sam had something serious to say and he felt it was more than talk about the ranch and general business concerns.

Finally, Sam told his story about the day's visit with the two political visitors from the East. Jake said, "Papa, I am surprised that you are even thinking about running for state senator. You never have had a good word for politicians. You know that Ida and I are very proud of you and we know you would do a good job. We would support you, but is this what you would really want to do?"

Rina suggested they meet every night that week and make a list of all the pros and cons of Sam getting into politics.

As Sam and Rina prepared for bed that night, Rina said, "Sam, you are a man with much pride and you know you are my favorite cowboy, and I have to say I have no doubt that you could do this job as a senator, but over the last year or so, you and I have aged a little. I have noticed you have slowed down a little physically. So, what I am concerned with is your health. Will this job affect your health too much? From what I have heard and read about the political world, it is a very tough lifestyle and I'm not sure it is for us."

Sam looked deep into Rina's eyes and said, "You are my life's partner and best friend and you know how I value your judgment. What you've just said is surely on my mind. I have also been reviewing our lifestyle. We have worked hard all our lives and we are beginning to really enjoy what we have. We are very comfortable financially. We have no serious worries or problems, so I'm wondering why we should change our lives so drastically?"

Rina answered, "I guess the one reason I think you should run for office would basically be to serve people, and Sam, I know you would be excellent at that job."

The next couple of weeks went by quickly and the family met every night.

Finally Sam broke his agreement about confidentiality. He decided he should meet with some close friends to get their reaction about his running for political office.

Rina and Sam invited the friends to dinner at the ranch. The highly trusted friends were Anna Dutman (widow of Cyrus), Dr. Herman Brown, and Willow and Lone Tall Tree.

After one of Rina's delightful dinners, Sam stood up, surprising his friends. This move was so unlike Sam. Sam then said, "I am standing because I am too nervous to sit."

Sam then told his story of the political group encouraging him to run for the office of state senator. After explaining the political situation, Sam then said, "I have a tough decision to make. Rina and I have pondered over this for many hours and we thought it was time to get some honest reactions from some true friends that we can trust."

For the next minute or so there was absolute silence. Then Rina spoke and said, "I know you are surprised, but please give us your honest feelings. This is such a huge undertaking for us to face."

Lone Tall Tree said, "Willow and I have told our people during election years that what we needed was someone like Sam

Rignez to represent us. We know you would lead us well. But, I'm not sure the lifestyle would be worth it for you. Our people have had so many bad experiences with worthless politicians, and Sam, the way I know you, you would not mix in too well with them. But, whatever you decide we'll support you all the way."

Everyone agreed with the Sioux leader and Dr. Brown said, "Nobody could have said it better."

These good friends agreed to work with Sam over the coming months if he decided to enter the political race.

A week later Sam sat down at the kitchen table with Rina and said, "I have made my decision about the political campaign."

Sam had many notes on the table before him. Sam added, "Rina, I've gone over all these notes many times and I've come to the conclusion that this political thing is just not for us. Right now it doesn't quite fit: I don't have a good feeling about this situation. Rina, as we both know, the West is rapidly changing in many ways. All the western towns are getting larger and with the growth there are new problems to face. I don't believe, at my age, that I can handle something like this. I actually think in our changing country and world that what is needed is younger people like our son Jake."

Sam went on to say to Rina, "This recent experience has set me to thinking about many things in a philosophical way. I have thought back about my old friend Cyrus Dutman who had some interesting ideas."

Sam added, "One time while we were riding on the range and talking about good times, Cyrus all of a sudden said that as we get older it is truly amazing what we learn in life. He had learned that there were times in life when it paid to be mistrustful of some men and situations. He had determined that there were evil people in this world that would do anything without thinking about how their actions would affect or hurt others. Because of memories and thoughts like these, I have decided to pass on political life."

Rina went to Sam and gave him a big hug and said, "I am relieved that you made your decision this way. I know how you studied this over so thoroughly and I think we'll be happier with the life we have."

The next day Sam contacted the political people who had made the proposal and told them of his decision. After they discussed Sam's decision, the politicians wished Sam well and said that they planned on keeping in close touch with him.

Thirty

or the next few weeks, Sam and Rina lived life at a relaxed pace. Rina said the previous month was just too fast and busy for their simple lifestyle. Then one day Rina said to Sam, "I'd like to get away for a few days. We have had a long, hard year and I'd like a little vacation time. Just you and me. I've been thinking, let's go back to Chicago and visit some old friends. You need a break also as you have worked very hard this past year."

Sam was completely surprised by Rina's idea, but after a minute of thinking it over, Sam thought it was a good idea.

Rina then said, "Sam, maybe you would like to take a trip to Europe to visit where you came from."

Sam replied, "Absolutely not! They might try to keep me there. You know how I love our country. I never want to leave it. Let's see what we can do to take a trip to Chicago and Wisconsin. I like that idea."

So, Sam and Rina made their plans for a long overdue vacation. They contacted Vito Rozzi, their friend and business acquaintance in Chicago, to make sure he would be at home while they were there. Next, they contacted Abel Zobel and his son Heimi in Wisconsin to arrange a visit with them also. The Zobels had developed their shoe and boot business into a very successful enterprise.

These good friends of Rina and Sam's welcomed them with a warm flourish that promised to be a fine get-together.

Because of all their busy schedules, they had not seen each other for a few years, but Sam did communicate with them regularly for business and on holidays.

Before they left on vacation Rina noticed that Sam was continually checking things over with Jake and Willy. Rina thought he was overdoing this and that made her nervous. Rina knew the problem—that Sam was worried that the ranch would not operate without him. So, Rina sat Sam down and scolded him, "Sam you know that Jake and Willy are very capable of handling everything. You are a workaholic, but you need to forget this place for a couple of weeks."

Sam and Rina boarded the early morning train and sat down in their Pullman bedroom suite for a leisurely trip east. They arrived in Chicago two days later where they were met at the station by Vito and Mara Rozzi, who gave them a big Windy City welcome.

For the next week Sam and Rina were wined and dined in some elegant restaurants. They also visited museums and were entertained at concerts and night clubs. Vito and Mara expressed their appreciation for all Rina and Sam had done in helping their nephew, Tony, become an artist and find his niche in life.

Time flew by quickly and Rina and Sam then drove north to visit their friends in the scenic part of southern Wisconsin. Again they received a hearty welcome and had a joyous time with their warm-hearted friends.

Rina and Sam were given a deluxe tour of the Zobel's shoe and boot plant. Sam was amazed at the operation which had been enlarged three times in the past few years. Business was truly blooming.

Abel patted Sam on the back and said, "Thanks to you for helping us get this whole thing off the ground. We will never forget you and what you have done for us over the years."

After another week of loafing and being treated royally, Sam began to get antsy and anxious to return to their ranch. Sam and Rina said their farewells to their friends and made a leisurely drive back to Chicago. They returned the rental car and caught the noon train for their return trip home.

Early the next morning Rina woke up and was surprised that Sam was not beside her. She dressed quickly and walked two cars back to the dining car where she found Sam talking to a black man. The man was evidently a chef as he was dressed in a white jacket and a chef's hat. After Sam introduced Rina to Ben, the chef, Ben politely excused himself and went back to the kitchen.

Rina scolded Sam for not telling her that he was leaving their sleeping room. Sam said, "I woke up early and wasn't feeling just right so I did not want to wake you. I then went to the dining car and met up with my new acquaintance, Ben."

Rina then quizzed Sam about not feeling right. Sam answered, "I had a stomachache and thought maybe it was something I ate. I seem okay now." They then returned to their sleeping room.

They spent the rest of the day napping and reading until it was time for dinner in the dining car.

Later that evening, Sam dozed off and Rina looked up from the book she was reading and noticed Sam had developed a very pained look on his face. She moved closer and found Sam sweating profusely. Rina got Sam to wake up and got him to mumble that he really felt ill and very uncomfortable in his abdominal area. Rina bathed his face with a wet cloth and ran out to find the conductor of the train.

Rina told the conductor her concern about Sam not feeling well. The conductor immediately checked his passenger roster to see if a doctor or a nurse were listed as passengers. The conductor and his assistant then went from car to car announcing the emergency need for a person with a medical background.

In the last car, a young woman raised her hand and waved to the conductor. The young woman told the conductor that her husband, who had just walked back to the dining car to get a cup of coffee, was a medical sergeant in the army.

They found the young sergeant and quickly went back to Sam and Rina's sleeping room. The sergeant checked Sam and from his limited medical knowledge knew that Sam was a very sick man and was in need of medical attention from a doctor. Then, surprisingly, Sam seemed to improve some. The sergeant stayed with Sam for quite a while to aid and comfort him.

The next train station was about forty miles down the line and the conductor used his emergency phone to call ahead and arrange for emergency assistance for Sam.

The train pulled into the next small town very early in the morning, where there was an ambulance ready to take Sam to the local hospital.

Sam and Rina were quickly driven to the emergency room and Sam was admitted. Two doctors and a nurse quickly began examining Sam and asking Rina questions They ordered several tests and administered a medication to ease the pain and help him rest.

The doctor met with Rina and said that Sam had symptoms of a severe abdominal disorder and it was possible a tumor was involved. It was recommended that Sam stay for another day under medication, after which he could travel home and receive medical attention from his family physician, Dr. Brown.

After another day in the small hospital, Sam and Rina boarded the train for home, about one hundred and twenty-five miles away.

Thirty-one

When they arrived at their hometown depot, Jake and Dr. Brown were there to meet them.

Again, Sam seemed to be feeling a little better. The pain and ill-feeling seemed to come quickly and then after a time would lessen. Sam was immediately taken to the hospital.

Dr. Brown informed Sam and Rina that a doctor friend of his, who was a specialist in abdominal problems, would be in town in a day or so. Dr. Brown would get his friend involved with Sam right away.

As he had planned, Dr. Brown's friend, Dr. Seinman, arrived two days later. Dr. Seinman, being a close friend of Dr. Brown's, made this trip once a year to share medical research. Dr. Brown said he also made the trip to explore and see more of the great plains area of the western part of the country.

The next day Dr. Seinman began his examination of Sam. Then the two doctors got together and shared their findings on Sam's illness. It was concluded that Sam's problem was a tumor and that they would use Dr. Seinman's expertise to perform the necessary surgery.

It was decided that Sam should rest and be under close observation for at least two days before the operation; the doctors felt that with medications and rest Sam would be stronger for the operation. He was quite weak and it was important for him to regain some of his strength before the ordeal of such a serious operation.

Two days later, Sam's condition took a turn for the worse. Almost overnight Sam's health dropped to a low level. Dr. Seinmar consulted with Dr. Brown and they knew an operation was out of the question. They administered a new so-called wonder drug that just might improve Sam's condition.

Unfortunately, after using the new medication, there was no improvement. Another biopsy was performed shortly after and the results indicated the tumor had grown. Sam was on continual medication and did not seem to get worse, but there was also no improvement.

Rina met with Dr. Brown to discuss Sam's prognosis. Being a friend of Rina and Sam, Dr. Brown had a difficult time discussing the situation with Rina. The good doctor told Rina, "We have done everything that we know of in dealing with cancer. It is a shame we did not know of Sam's problem earlier. In my previous examinations of Sam he had never complained of any symptoms of this illness. At this time all we can do is keep Sam as comfortable as possible. It is unknown how long Sam will be able to keep up his fight against this monstrous disease."

Dr. Brown added, "We just do not have the ability to find a cure for this disease. I'm sorry to say this to you Rina, but all we can do now is to help Sam fight the pain. You and Sam will have to decide about where Sam should be—here in the hospital or at your ranch."

Rina said, "Sam would want to return to the ranch as soon as possible. I know he wants to spend as much time as possible at his ranch and see as many more beautiful sunsets as he can."

Arrangements were made for Sam to return to the ranch. Sam said to his friend, Dr. Brown, jokingly as he was leaving, "Doc, don't expect me back too soon. I have a lot of work and catching up to do at the ranch."

As Dr. Brown turned and went back into the hospital, two nurses noticed the good doctor wiping away tears after Sam's attempt at some humor with his old friend.

Thirty-two

When Sam and Rina got home, all the ranch hands and some close friends were there to welcome him home. Sam, of course, was extremely happy to see all the good people.

Rina quietly mentioned to the group that Sam was going to need a nap very soon because it had been an exciting day for him and he was very tired. Everyone understood and soon they all headed out after the brief visit with their friend.

Everything in the ranch house was set up to make life easier for Sam to get around. Rina rented a hospital bed to make him more comfortable. He could walk, but very slowly.

After being home a few days, Sam told Rina, "I want to take a ride and look over the pastures and check out some broken fences."

Rina put her foot down and talked Sam out of riding his horse. Instead, Rina got Willy and Jake to get their old ranch wagon out so Sam could get out and enjoy his prairie trails.

Rina prepared a small snack to take with them on their enjoyable ride across the prairie. Rina knew that Sam was in pain, but the wagon ride seemed to perk him up and bring a smile and glow to his face.

When they returned to the ranch house Sam said to Rina, "Let's do this again tomorrow. But, let's do it at early evening and watch the sunset."

For the next few days, Sam and Rina went for short wagon rides in the evening. Sam started calling this excursion *Sam's Sunset Special* or the "SSS" tour.

As the days passed, Rina noticed that Sam was getting more tired each day. Rina contacted Dr. Brown about her concern and he came to check on Sam.

The doctor asked Sam about the pain that he was having and if the medication was giving him any relief. Rina spoke up and told the doctor that Sam never complained about pain, but she knew at times the pain was severe.

The doctor then gave Sam a different medication that was more potent. He also warned Rina that Sam should not overuse this new potent medication.

In a few days, Sam told her that he would skip their sunset ride for that day. Right away she had a bad feeling about Sam's comment.

Rina remembered Dr. Brown telling her to prepare herself for Sam's decline in physical abilities. The next day, after preparing their breakfast, Rina went to their bedroom to walk Sam out to the kitchen.

He was still in bed staring out the window as he looked out at the eastern horizon and the rising sun.

Rina went over and sat beside her old cowboy and told him to join her for breakfast. Sam reached over to her and wrapped his arms around his beautiful and loving wife. With a low tremor in his voice, Sam told Rina, "I'm not hungry; I just can't eat right now."

Sam then laid down and said he would take a little nap and then he might feel like eating. Rina noticed that Sam was immediately fast asleep.

Two hours later Rina returned to check on Sam. He was still fast asleep. Rina wiped Sam's face with a cold, damp cloth and this slowly woke Sam up from his deep sleep.

Rina placed her arm behind Sam's shoulder to help him out of bed, but Sam's body would not react. Rina helped Sam to a sitting position and told him she would bring his breakfast to him.

Rina quickly brought in a hearty breakfast on a tray. Sam slowly picked at his breakfast. He forced himself to eat more than he could really handle as he did not want to hurt Rina's feelings by not eating. Finally, Sam gave up on eating and told Rina he would finish it later. Sam then rolled over to take another nap.

Rina went to the kitchen and called Dr. Brown. She told the doctor that she was very concerned as Sam seemed to be slipping and she did not know what to do to help him.

The doctor arrived at the ranch within an hour. Sam was still sleeping and the doctor said he was sure the change in medication was what caused Sam to sleep so much.

Sam slowly woke up and Dr. Brown examined him and then decided it would be wise to put Sam in the hospital for a more thorough examination.

Jake and Willy helped Sam get into their car and Jake drove them to the hospital. He was admitted to a private room and immediately fell asleep. Dr. Brown told Rina she should go back to the ranch and get some rest as he was concerned about her health due to her constant caring for Sam. Rina refused to go home and Dr. Brown drove her to his home where his wife, Eda, sat with Rina for a time. Soon Rina went to bed for some much needed rest.

Meanwhile, Jake sat at Sam's bedside for a couple of hours and then went home. He planned to return early the next morning.

Over the next two days, Sam's vital signs slowed down more and more. On the third day a terrible storm blew into the area with a very cold wind and lots of rain. Rina and Jake were with Sam the entire day. In the early evening, Jake encouraged his mother to go to Dr. Brown's house and get a few hours of rest.

Jake sat by his father, watching him waste away and wishing he could somehow help Sam fight his illness. Sam, in his dreamworld due to heavy medication, would start mumbling—

sometimes in German, sometimes in Yiddish, and sometimes in English. This was all frightening and frustrating for Jake.

Jake went to a nurse and told her of his concern. Just then Maria Cardoza came on duty and went immediately to Jake and the nurse. Maria, a highly respected nurse, said that she would help Jake since she was an old friend of the family.

Maria went with Jake to Sam's room and after checking his chart, she told Jake that Sam should settle down soon from his latest medication. Maria then left Jake and told him she would be nearby if he needed her.

Thirty-three

Jake sat by Sam's bedside thinking of all the wonderful experiences he had shared with his father. Jake thought of this good man and what a strong, powerful person he had always been. So now, it was hard to watch him slip away before his eyes. Sam had been a strong individual who had played a great part in working to expand and see America grow.

Suddenly Sam raised his head and spoke to Jake. Jake got up and went to Sam. Sam reached out to Jake and pulled him down close.

Sam's voice was very low and weak as he put his hands around Jake's neck, pulling him closer. In his low voice Sam said, "I have something to tell you. Please stay close to me for a few minutes. Over the years I've told you many things about our family. But there are some things I haven't told you. Your mother and I decided it was not necessary some years ago to tell you certain things about our family. But recently I have changed my mind. A man should know and is entitled to know his family background."

Sam added, "So, my Jacob, I'll share my story with you. It isn't something bad, it is just something that happened. Something that happened years ago when things were much different. What I'm about to tell you took place years ago and I don't think it could happen today. Our country has changed, our rules and laws have changed. People in general live and think differently today."

Sam, after a brief pause continued with his tale, "So, bear with me and I will tell you what I must."

Jake could not imagine what Sam was talking about.

Sam then went on, "Some years ago your mother and I traveled back to Philadelphia. We were doing well on our ranch after putting in a lot of hard work. But we had to return to that city because there was a terrible tragedy with some dear friends of ours that compelled us to return to help them with their suffering. In our absence, our faithful friend, Willy, took care of the ranch.

The thing is that our dear friends, Dan and Lela Favenger, both passed away a few months of each other. Sadly, this left their son, Jerald, an orphan.

At this point tears were rolling down Sam's cheeks and he was having trouble speaking. Jake was worried that his talking might be too much for his father in his weakened condition.

Sam continued, "Jacob, listen closely because now I'll tell you a confusing part of my story. On our trip East, our young son, Jacob, became very ill." Sam sensed the confused look on Jake's face. "Please be patient and bear with me. When we arrived in Philadelphia with the help of our friends the Weidmans, and their family doctor, we got Jacob settled in the hospital. Our Jacob's illness had become quite severe at this point. Then the tragedy of our lives came. After a few days, our young son's frail body couldn't overcome his illness and he passed on to God's hands. Such a sadness came into our lives. I worried that your mother would never recover from our loss.

"You obviously know that the Jacob I mentioned was a different Jacob. At the time, and with much confusion while we were in Philadelphia, the death of our friends, the loss of our son, and young Jerald becoming an orphan, we prayed and prayed and finally made a decision. Jerald was without parents, we had lost our son who was an only child, and Grandfather Favinger was quite elderly and in poor health. Other family members did not seem able or interested in taking on another child."

Sam paused and then continued, "So, after discussing the situation with old Mr. Favinger, we decided to make young Jerald a member of our family. The youngster, in a sense, became our Jacob. By doing this it solved a problem for many of us. A small lost boy found a home and new parents, and a loving couple found a lost son."

Then Sam added, "We left Philadelphia quickly for the ranch because we did not want any entanglements with authorities over our adding Jerald to our family. Jake, you have probably guessed by now what I am trying to tell you. You, my Jacob, are that boy who lost his parents and became our son."

Sam caught his breath and continued saying, "In the beginning because you were only two years old, I know how confusing everything was for you. Your mother, Rina, showered you with her love and as the days and months passed you became more adjusted to ranch life and our prairie country and wonderful people. Many times we discussed whether to tell you of your real parents, our dear friends, but during those early years a glorious relationship developed between us. Rina said at that time that God sent one of his angels down to guide you to us after our sad losses. But Jake, as time went by we just put this problem aside and truly looked at you as our son Jacob. We did not think we were harming you in any way. Please, please forgive us for keeping this from you for so long. For the last year or so I thought more and more that it was time to tell you about your young life. Simply put, a man should know these things. Jacob, my son, I love you with all my heart."

By this time, with tears streaming down his face, Jake was truly overcome. Jake leaned closer to Sam and said, "Papa, don't feel bad. As you told me what happened I could see you were in pain explaining it to me. I will have many questions about my other family—a family I remember nothing about. But Papa, you are my father, I love you and will love you forever and ever."

At that moment, Rina walked in the door and when she looked at the two of them she knew what had happened. She went to Sam and said, "Sam, you told Jake, didn't you? I knew you wanted to do this. I am glad Jake now knows."

Rina then moved to Jake and they embraced each other. Rina said, "Jake, forgive us for keeping this part of your life from you, but at the time, we were very confused and thought we did the best thing."

Jake then said to Sam and Rina, "Please don't feel guilty. I look at you both as my parents and love you very much. We are a family and nothing will change that. Thank you Papa and Momma for telling me about what happened many years ago."

The evening's talk with Jake had tired Sam considerably. Rina could see this and suggested Sam get some rest. Sam said good night, rolled over on his side, and went to sleep.

Thirty-four

arly the next morning, Rina and Jake were just returning to the hospital, and after parking the car, Rina reached for Jake's elbow and said, "Jake, look at that beautiful sunrise. I don't think I have ever seen a sunrise so glorious. Let's help Sam get to a window to see it."

They went to Sam's room. Just as they approached the door, Dr. Brown and Maria opened the door. Rina and the doctor looked each other in the eye and Rina immediately noticed that Dr. Brown's face was white as the snow in a prairie snowstorm.

The good doctor reached for Rina and said, "Sam just left us—only ten minutes ago. I had just checked him over and he said, "Dr. Braunstein, I think I'll take a short nap before breakfast. He would call me Dr. Braunstein off and on to create a little of Sam's humor. Then Sam rolled over, gasped as if trying to take a deep breath, and my dear friend quietly left us."

Dr. Brown added, "Rina and Jake, I am sorry to have to tell this—it is a loss to many of us."

Maria, fighting back tears, went to Rina and helped her to Sam's side. Rina and Jake sat with Sam for the next hour while Dr. Brown made final arrangements for Sam's departure from the hospital.

The next day, after a sleepless night, Rina and Jake sat down to plan Sam's funeral. They planned a ceremony that would not be lengthy, which was Sam's wish. Sam had previously told Rina that when his final day came he would like a funeral similar to his friend Cyrus Dutman's, as it had impressed Sam. Then after the ceremony, Sam wanted to be taken to his final resting place in an old ranch wagon pulled by two of their Belgian workhorses.

Willow Tall Tree and her children volunteered to dress up the wagon with some beautiful flowers.

Rina told Jake and his wife, Ida, "During the past year Sam and I had discussed our last days a few times. We thought that as we got older we should make a few plans and not leave any big problems for you. Sam's biggest request was that he wanted his final resting place to be here at the ranch. I feel obligated to keep this promise to Sam. That resting place is about four hundred yards west of the house. In that area there is a rise on the land, a knoll that we used to ride to and watch the beautiful sunsets. It's a favorite, peaceful place of Sam's. So, that is where we will lay him to rest."

Two days later Sam's funeral was held in the Lutheran Church near the center of town. Sam was not a devout church member, but he supported several denominations regularly with financial assistance. The local minister called Sam, "the man of all seasons and all faiths."

Many people cared deeply for Sam. Over the years he did many things for many people in the area without any fanfare. And on the last day, the day of his final departure from the earth and great plains, many, many friends overflowed the church. People were even lined up outside the church. A communication system was set up so that the words of tribute could be heard by all the friends outside the church.

After the ceremony, Sam's casket was placed on the old ranch wagon for a last ride to his final resting place. Sam's old and faithful friend and ranch foreman, Willy Gorman, drove the handsomely decorated wagon through the streets of the town. The procession slowly made its way to the Rignez ranch.

In the history of this small city, no one had ever experienced a gathering or tribute such as this. The large flow of people followed the old wagon out to the knoll west of the ranch house. The crowd was scattered all over the prairie rise and small hillside to honor their friend.

The minister said his final blessing and then Dr. Brown made a few remarks and told the gathering of friends to read the humble words carved on a large hardwood plaque at the head of the grave site. On the plaque words in memory of Samuel had been carved by Lone Tall Tree and read as follows:

Here Lies Our Friend
Samuel Rignez

A man who won the respect of all.
A man who loved the land.
A man who found the good in all others.
A man who is leaving our world a better place.
A man who truly is our man of all seasons.

Thirty-five

As the service ended there was a deep silence over the prairie. The silence remained for several minutes. Then out of respect and friendship for Rina, the hundreds of people took a last look at Sam's resting place and walked away, heading back to town or their farms and ranches.

All of a sudden came the tune, "Taps," from a trumpet on a nearby hill next to the grave site. Playing the trumpet was Joe Cardoza, a family friend who was home on leave from the army. The people who were walking stopped and sadly listened until the last note.

Rina's faith and inner strength carried her through the remainder of this sad day.

The next day Willow Tall Tree and her youngest daughter came to the ranch to stay and comfort her for the next few days.

Then Rina asked Jake to come to the ranch for a family talk. Rina's main reason for the talk was to give some guidance to her son and also a lot of encouragement during this stressful time.

Rina said, "Jake, you know our ranch and much of our business interests, but there are some things I need to tell you.

"I think your father taught you many things and he taught you well. First of all, and you know this, we have done well with our ranch and also some other business ventures that Sam had helped develop."

Rina then added, "I know many things were successful because of Sam's character. Jake, I believe your father was a real expert when it came to working with people. Some people I have known through your father have even told me he was a genius in this field of dealing with people. Jake, in our small world of success you now have a great challenge and opportunity ahead of you. You, Jake, are the man and the driving force of our operation. You have learned many things from your father, but don't ever think you have to be Sam."

"So, Jake," Rina continued, "one thing Sam learned as a young man was that you never really understand a person until you consider things from his point of view. It is important to learn to have compassion for others. There are many, many, good people that we have dealt with in our lifetime. People that we truly want to know in our lives. But there are some other people in life that are not good to deal with. We have told you stories of some of these undesirables. I mention this only to remind you to be aware of those who appear questionable in their actions and requests to you."

After a short pause Rina continued, "My son, your father will always be with us and I'll always share with you what I feel he and I believe. Please tell me what I can do to help with whatever concerns you have. With the passing of your father we are also seeing the last of one of those strong individualistic men who worked to make our great plains area what it is today. There aren't many of those old-timer cowboys left."

It was early evening and Rina said with a catch in her voice, "Jake, let's take a little walk and watch another one of our beautiful sunsets."

About the Author

Jerry Eberly grew up in western Nebraska in Alliance. He attended Doane College for two years and graduated from LaVerne University, LaVerne, California.

Eberly had a thirty-year career with the YMCA in Pasadena, California, Green Bay, Wisconsin, and Minot, North Dakota.

In growing up, he always enjoyed family stories being told by his parents and older relatives. Over the years he kept notes of the many tales told by family members—all the way from Europe to the prairie in western Nebraska. Finally, a few family members and friends urged him to write some of these interesting experiences and *Sam's Journey* is the result.

Eberly and his wife Marilyn are the parents of two daughters and three sons.

Eberly, all through his life, has had strong feelings for Nebraska and finally returned to spend his retirement years in Lincoln, Nebraska.